AN ANGEL FO

Riverbend, Texas Heat 5

Marla Monroe

MENAGE EVERLASTING

Siren Publishing, Inc.
www.SirenPublishing.com

A SIREN PUBLISHING BOOK
IMPRINT: Ménage Everlasting

AN ANGEL FOR THEM
Copyright © 2013 by Marla Monroe

ISBN: 978-1-62740-380-1

First Printing: July 2013

Cover design by Les Byerley
All art and logo copyright © 2013 by Siren Publishing, Inc.

Printed in the U.S.A.

PUBLISHER
Siren Publishing, Inc.
www.SirenPublishing.com

AN ANGEL FOR THEM

Riverbend, Texas Heat 5

MARLA MONROE
Copyright © 2013

Chapter One

Travis Woods slowed his truck to keep from hitting the garbage on the side of the road. Why did people insist on dumping their trash along the highway? It didn't make sense to him. If it hadn't been drizzling rain, he would get out and throw it in the back of his truck, but he didn't really want to get wet. He passed the bag of garbage about the time that it moved. He slammed on the brakes and stopped. It was a good thing no one was behind him or he would have caused a wreck.

Had it been the wind that had moved the stuff or was there actually something alive in the bag? The idea that someone had put out a puppy or kitten on the side of the road in the rain angered him. He squinted into his passenger side mirror to see if it moved again. It did.

He quickly pulled over to the side of the road and climbed out of his truck. He carefully approached the bundle of whatever it was in case there could be a stray dog or even a coyote rummaging around in the trash bag. Instead, when he drew closer he saw that it was a person huddled with the garbage bag covering their body.

"Hey, you okay? Do you need help?"

The bag jerked and a pair of legs emerged to scamper back from him. It settled well back from the road and huddled once again. From the size of the bag and the mass bundled up in it, he figured it had to be a child or maybe a small woman. He couldn't leave them on the side of the road in the rain.

He carefully edged closer but stopped when the bag began to shake.

"Let me help you. I'll give you a ride wherever you want to go. Maybe back to town?"

The bag slowly stood up but didn't move closer. He smiled and held out his hand.

"Come on. You can ride in the backseat if you feel better that way. I won't hurt you. Do you want to go back to town?"

A soft and definitely feminine voice spoke up for the first time. "Is there a shelter there?"

"Yes, there's a shelter in Riverbend. Do you want me to take you there?" he asked.

"Please. I don't have anywhere to go. He just put me out and told me to walk."

"Well, let's get you out of this rain and into the truck first. Then you can tell me what happened."

She hesitated for a second then sighed as if all hope was lost to her. She slowly walked toward him. The tiny woman appeared completely dejected by the way she slumped forward. He felt nothing but sorrow for her. She finally made it over to stand in front of him. Then she looked up from beneath the garbage bag and his heart nearly stopped. She had the prettiest light-blue eyes he had ever seen. Sad blue eyes, but gorgeous just the same. They seemed to look right through him and into his heart.

"Thanks. I was too tired to walk any further."

All he could do was nod and lead her to his truck. When they made it to the door, she stopped and seemed to contemplate where she wanted to ride. Finally she moved to the front of the truck and started to open the door. Travis snapped out of his daze and quickly opened the door for her. She pulled off the garbage bag and dropped it on the ground. He was so bedazzled by her head of golden-red hair that he didn't even bother to pick it up and throw it in the back of the truck.

Her hair was just as pretty as her eyes. Even wet and tangled, nothing could hide the truth of how amazing it would be dry and combed out. It hung in sodden clumps around her shoulders, reaching just below her shoulder blades. He ached to reach out and touch it, but he restrained himself since that would surely send her screaming in the opposite direction of him and the truck.

With a bit of effort, he managed to close the door without touching her. Then he circled around the front of the truck and climbed in the cab. He pulled a blanket from the backseat and handed it to her. Then he put the truck in drive and turned around in the middle of the road to head back to town even though all he wanted to do was take her home where he and his brother Randy could take care of her. His brother would flip at seeing her in the shape she was in. They treasured women and would never allow one to get into the sort of trouble she seemed to have found herself.

"I'm Travis Woods. My brother, Randy, and I own a ranch outside of town. Would you tell me your name?"

"Angela Carter. My name is Angela. Thanks for helping me."

"That's a pretty name, Angela. I don't mind helping you one bit." He glanced over at where she sat huddled near the door, hanging on to the blanket and the seat belt like a lifesaver. "Want to tell me what happened?"

"My boyfriend decided he didn't want to be saddled with me anymore and put me out on the Interstate. I knew better than to walk there, so I took the first exit I came to, and here I am."

"I can't imagine any sane person just dumping you in the rain on the side of the road. That's plain criminal."

"It wasn't raining yesterday."

Travis almost slammed on the brakes again. He turned and looked at her then back at the road.

"You've been walking since yesterday? Where did you sleep? Have you even had anything to eat?"

"I slept in an old abandoned car back a ways before I took this road. It was dry and wasn't too dirty. That's where I found that plastic bag. I haven't had anything to eat since yesterday morning when we had peanut butter and crackers."

"Honey, we'll get you something to eat first, and then I'll take you where they can help you get cleaned up. There should be somewhere you can work so you can move out of the shelter pretty quickly.

"I'm really good with numbers. I used to work as a bookkeeper for a little store where I'm from."

"Where are you from, Angela?"

"Belzoni, Mississippi."

"Never heard of it. Was it a big town?"

"No, just a little place that's known for catfish farming. When I graduated from high school, I got a scholarship to a junior college in Moorhead and got my two-year degree in business." She smiled, and it brightened her entire face.

"Then you shouldn't have any trouble finding a job. In fact, we have a need for a bookkeeper out at our farm. You might want to think about that." Travis couldn't believe his luck. The woman of his dreams had fallen into his lap and she could possibly run their office for them.

He and Randy had been looking for someone to take over the everyday office duties for a while now. Unfortunately there weren't a lot of qualified people out there in a small town the size of Riverbend, Texas. Most everyone had a job that wanted one, and that meant that all the bookkeepers and such were employed.

"Oh, that sounds nice, but don't you need references? I can give you the name of the store I used to work in, but they weren't too happy about me leaving all of a sudden."

"Why did you leave?"

"Well, my parents died while I was in school, and I didn't have anywhere to live. The house wasn't paid for so the bank eventually took it back. I couldn't afford to make the payment and go to school, too. I had to pay for the bus to go to and from school and food and such." She waved her hand. "Anyway, after graduation I decided I could do better in a bigger city, so I took the bus to Jackson, and looked for a job. I never expected it would be so hard to find one in a city that large, but I finally found one at a fast-food joint. It didn't pay much, but it kept a roof over my head and enough food to keep from starving."

"I guess you were a little overwhelmed by a place that size."

"Yeah, it was hard to find a place cheap enough to rent that was clean. I ended up in a not-so-nice part of town. At least the apartment was decent enough, and it wasn't far from where I worked. I could walk from the bus stop. Anyway, that's how I met Phil, my ex-boyfriend. He started talking to me at the bus stop one day and we started seeing each other."

"So how did you end up in this part of Texas? I mean it's a long way from Mississippi." Travis pulled into town and parked in front of the Riverbend Diner.

"He moved in with me to save on rent. I thought we were doing okay, but one day he decided we should move to somewhere nicer and find better jobs. He was working as a short-order cook in a truck stop during the day and played in a band at night. He said he had an offer to play in a bigger band in Phoenix that would mean more money. I was stupid enough to think he loved me and wanted me to go with him. All he wanted was my money to buy the car and get as close to Arizona as he could. Then he said he didn't want to be burdened with someone like me."

"Someone like you? What in the hell was that supposed to mean?"

"Someone who didn't fit into his world, his music world. I don't have a musical bone in my body."

He turned and looked at her in amazement. She was beautiful from the glorious crown of golden-red hair to her generous breasts and gently rounded ass. Her eyes were mesmerizing, and he couldn't stop thinking about holding her, kissing her. He just knew Randy would feel the same way about her.

"Let's get you something to eat. You have to be starved."

Angela's stomach growled and they both laughed even though her face turned a cute shade of pink.

He helped her out of the truck then opened the door of the diner and steered her toward his favorite booth in back.

The waitress, Jillian, walked over with a smile. "Hi, Travis, what can I get you guys?"

"Angela? What do you want to drink?"

"Just water please. I'm really thirsty."

"Same here. Might want to bring a pitcher."

Jillian furrowed her brows but didn't ask questions. She nodded and walked off. When she returned, she set two glasses in front of them before pouring their water.

"Do you know what you want, or do you need a few minutes?" she asked.

"What's the special today, Jill?" Travis asked.

"Meatloaf, potatoes, and green beans."

"Sound good to you, Angela?"

"Yes please." She smiled a shy smile at Jill.

"One special and a burger with fries for me." Travis felt his cell phone vibrate against his hip.

He pulled it off his belt holder and noted it was Randy.

"Excuse me, Angela. It's my brother. I better see what he needs."

He answered the phone. "Yeah, what's up Randy?"

"Where are you? I thought you were on your way home?"

"I got sidetracked. Is something wrong?" He smiled over at Angela, who was studiously looking around the diner.

"Sidetracked? That doesn't sound like you."

"I'll be another hour. I'll talk to you about it when I get home."

"Hmm, okay. Guess I have to wait 'til you get back. You obviously can't talk right now."

"Nope. I'll see you later." He pushed the end button and stuck the phone back in its holder.

"I hope everything is okay there." Angela's pretty voice vibrated along his already-aching cock.

"Everything's just fine."

The waitress brought their food, and Travis watched as Angela tried to keep from inhaling it. She would start to stuff her mouth then stop and slowly take a bite before putting her fork back down while she chewed. If it hadn't broken his heart, it would have been amusing. All he could think about was her out in the rain with a garbage bag covering her head, and it made him mad enough to spit nails. If he ever saw that Phil guy...

"So what do you raise on your ranch? Just cows or do you have horses, too?"

Travis smiled. "We raise cows for beef, but we have horses to ride and even a few goats."

"Goats? Do you have chickens and hogs?" Her eyes grew round as she took another bite of her food.

"No. They're too much trouble since we don't need them for food. The goats are sort of a long story. They were going to be put down because the owner died. We were buying his land and the family didn't want to be bothered with them. My brother couldn't see letting them be killed just because no one wanted to have to deal with them."

Her eyes softened. "That was really nice of y'all to do that. Goats can be worrisome to say the least."

"You can say that again. We didn't know anything about them when we hauled them over to our place. Suffice it to say we've learned a lot in the last year that we've had them."

She actually giggled before taking a drink of her water. He refilled the now-empty glass and was glad they had the pitcher close at hand. She'd almost drained it as well. Knowing that she had been that thirsty tore him up inside. No one should have to go hungry or thirsty, ever, especially around Riverbend, Texas.

"Thank you for the meal, Travis. I really appreciate it. I'll pay you back as soon as I get a job." She straightened in her chair and wiped her mouth with her napkin.

"How about dessert?" He really wasn't ready to hand her off to Helen at the shelter yet.

"Goodness. I'd love to try something, but I'm really too full. I'll make myself sick."

"Can't have you getting sick." He signaled for the waitress. "I'll have a piece of your apple pie to go and the check."

Jillian smiled and hurried off. She returned with a boxed-up piece of pie and Mattie, the diner's owner in tow.

"Hey, Travis. How's Randy doing?" Mattie asked.

"Doing fine. He's back at the ranch. How are you and your husbands doing? You look mighty fine."

"Oh, those two are right as rain. Giving me fits about taking more time off all the time." She looked over at his guest. "Who do we have here? Don't reckon I've seen you around here before, sweetie."

"This is Angela Carter. She's just arrived in Riverbend." Travis smiled at the pretty woman across from him.

"Good to meet you, Angela. My husbands and I run this place. It's good to have you here. If you're looking for work, I might have some part time available. You just let me know."

"Oh, no you don't, Mattie. I've already talked to her about helping us with our books out on the ranch. You're not sweet-talking my help away from me." Travis almost panicked and hoped he didn't sound rude. No way was he letting Angela get away from them before they had even had a chance to get to know her.

"You devil you. I ought to sic Bruce on you for getting the jump on me." Mattie's eyes twinkled as she took the money he held out for the check.

"Thank you both so much for the kind offers. I'll think about both of them." She looked from one to the other with worry evident in her expression.

"Now don't worry about it, sweetie. Travis knows I'm joking with him. If you have a chance to work out at the ranch, you should jump at it since it will be more money and more hours than what I can give you right now." Mattie winked at her.

"Ready to go, Angela?" Travis stood up and helped her from her chair.

Picking up the box Jillian had handed him, he waved good-bye as they walked toward the door. Travis opened the door for her, following Angela outside. When they emerged from the diner it was to find that the rain had nearly stopped. A light drizzle fell on them as Travis opened the door to his truck for Angela to climb in. Her ratty jeans were pretty much threadbare as was the thin blouse that had already dampened from the quick walk to his truck.

Travis hurried around the front of the truck and jumped in. He hated leaving her at the boarding house he'd told her was a shelter, but he didn't know what else to do right then. He was sure she would never agree to go home with him when she knew nothing about him and his brother. Plus, he needed to talk to Randy about her first. And he wanted to ready a place for her to move into so she would be closer to them.

"Here is the shelter. It's a nice enough place to stay. Helen Causey runs it. She'll take good care of you here." He parked the truck out front, but instead of opening the door, he turned toward her. "I'm serious about the job, Angela. We could really use someone who knows how to run an office and handle the books. We've needed someone for quite some time, but there's no one around here with any experience."

"Thanks for the offer. I won't say no 'cause I need a job, but how do you know you can trust me? I mean you don't know anything about me yet."

"You're right. I don't know anything about you, but my gut instinct says I can trust you. It's never steered me wrong before. Get settled in with Helen and we can talk more tomorrow. I'll bring my brother out tomorrow afternoon and we'll talk more about the job. Why don't you tell me who I can call back in Belzoni and I'll talk to them before we come to meet with you?" Travis asked.

"That sounds fair enough. Do you have anything in here I can write the information on?"

Travis reached over and opened the glove compartment. Pulling out a notepad, he closed it again and handed it to her along with the pen he carried in his shirt pocket. He watched as she wrote down the information in a careful and precise handwriting before handing it to him.

"Great. Let's get you settled with Helen." Travis opened his door and walked around the truck to help Angela down.

When they walked inside the small building housed next to the sheriff's office and combined police station, Helen greeted them with a welcoming smile. Just like that, Angela was pulled from his grasp, and he was dismissed. Just as quickly as she'd come into his world, Helen had snatched her back out. Hopefully, it would only be for a couple of nights. Something told him that Angela was the woman he and his brother had been waiting for.

Travis quickly explained that Angela needed a safe place to stay for a few days, emphasizing that she had requested a shelter so Helen would understand. Although she took in the occasional needy person, she mostly ran the place as a boarding house. It wouldn't do for Angela to learn that just yet. She'd never accept a room or help from the woman if she knew the complete truth.

He climbed up in the truck and turned it toward home. He and Randy had a lot of talking to do. He just hoped Randy was in a better place than he had been of late. He was afraid his brother was giving up on their dream of sharing a woman between them and living in a family like they'd grown up in. He was sure that once he met Angela though, he would realize that dreams did come true.

Chapter Two

Angela let Helen lead her to the storeroom where they located several changes of clothes and toiletries before climbing a set of stairs to the second floor. Then she led her a short ways down the hall where she unlocked a door and opened it for Angela to go inside.

"It's not very large, but it has a comfortable bed and chest with a mirror. The bathroom is through there. You share it with the room next to you, but there's no one in it right now, so you have it to yourself. I only have two men living here right now. Both are good men and work at the lumberyard in town. You can lock your door though if you feel better that way."

Angela smiled but didn't know what to say. The woman had a way of just bulldozing through everything. Her pretty light-brown hair was pulled back in a small bun and she had the sweetest face Angela had ever seen. Her hazel eyes held a deep kindness that drew Angela in with a glance. She doubted she would ever be able to keep a secret from this woman. Not that she had any to keep.

"This is really nice, Helen. Thank you for letting me stay here for a few days. I just need to get a job and find a place I can afford."

"No problem, honey. You can stay here as long as you like. That's why it's here." She hugged Angela. "Now, why don't you get a shower and changed into something warmer. We have two meals a day, breakfast and dinner. They're simple meals, but you can eat your fill. Keep your room and the bathroom clean, and you can come and go as you like. Since you're a woman, I would prefer if you would let me know if you are going to be late so I don't have to send the sheriff out looking for you. We look out for each other here in Riverbend."

Angela nodded. "I will. Travis and his brother are supposed to come over tomorrow afternoon sometime to talk to me about a job. I hope that is okay."

"That's fine. They're good men. They've helped over the years to keep this place in good shape. You're welcome to come downstairs anytime you want some company. Dinner tonight will be at six." With that, Helen turned and walked back through the door.

Angela closed it behind the woman, and after staring at the knob for a few seconds, she locked it. The room was small but comfortable looking. Everything looked almost brand new, and it was clean. She sorted through the clothes they'd brought up and put them away in the chest, leaving out a change for when she finished her shower. She couldn't wait to clean up. After spending the night in that car and getting wet, she felt like something the cat had dragged in.

The bathroom was really quite nice considering it was shared between two rooms. She found that the hot water worked great and allowed herself to drift as she washed off. So much had happened in the space of a couple of hours that she wasn't sure how to process it all. The main thing on her mind was Travis Woods. Not only had he rescued her off the side of the road, but he'd fed her and taken her to the shelter like he had promised. The fact that he hadn't tried to take her home with him or even attack her in his truck went a long ways to making him a true hero in her book.

The added bonus of a possible job was icing on the cake. She was deeply thankful for what the good Lord had given her. It was up to her now to make something of it. She would do her best to make the most of the gift. Now if only she could manage to earn enough to rent a small room somewhere safe. She knew nothing of the area, but she was sure Helen would be able to direct her when the time came. It would take several months to earn enough to set up in a small apartment.

As she toweled dry, her thoughts turned to how good Travis looked. He was way out of her class, but he made excellent eye candy for someone like her. With his dark-brown hair that was just short of being shaggy and those amazing chocolate eyes, Angela thought she would embarrass herself by staring at him like a lovesick schoolgirl. Fortunately her stomach had outvoted her eyes and she'd concentrated on her meal for the most part. Still, she'd snuck several quick looks at how his smile warmed his face and took away the harsh lines that had been apparent when he'd first found her. Even the small scar at the corner of his left eye didn't detract from his handsome face.

When he'd helped her into the truck both times, she'd marveled at his strength. He appeared to be about six foot three inches of hard muscle. He would have to be to have almost picked her up. She wasn't a small woman despite having fallen on lean times. She knew she was a little curvier than most men liked. And her butt was anything but small.

She figured he must spend a great deal of time outside working since his skin still held on to a solid tan even though they were on the back end of winter and knocking on spring's door. She wondered just how far that tan went on his body. She closed her eyes and shook her head.

Best to get those kinds of thoughts out of my head right now. If he ends up being one of my bosses, I have no business imagining him without clothes.

Angela snorted and pulled on the new-looking jeans and blouse. It wasn't like she had a chance at catching his eye anyway. They were respectable men, and she was a homeless woman without a cent to her name with nothing but the clothes she'd been given out of the generosity of others. She figured in their world she was one step up from trailer trash.

With that cheerful thought, she decided a nap would help her recover from the last few days. She hadn't slept much at all last night being out in the open as she'd been. Every noise had her eyes snapping open in fear. She quickly dried her hair with the blow dryer that was provided in the bathroom and brushed it out so it wouldn't get tangled while she rested.

She eased down on the bed and found that the mattress felt just like new. She sighed as she curled her feet under the covers and closed her eyes. She couldn't wait to find out more about the job Travis had talked about. She prayed that her boss in Belzoni wouldn't ruin her chances at landing the position. She really could use the chance.

* * * *

Travis all but ran up the steps to the porch once he got home. He couldn't wait to talk to Randy about Angela and his offer of a job. He clutched the sheet of paper that had the name and phone number of her boss from her last job in his hand. As long as the other man didn't accuse her of theft or something equally as bad, he planned to hire her.

When he closed the door behind him, Randy stuck his head out of the office door just off to the side of the staircase. More than likely he was sitting in the desk chair and had rolled it across the room. He tended to roll it around the room instead of getting up and walking. Travis had no idea why since he knew his brother didn't have a lazy bone in him, but he chalked it up to one of the crazy things that made up Randy.

"Hey. I'm in here. What kept you an extra hour in town, brother?" Randy's head disappeared back into the other room.

Travis knew he was grinning like a crazy person, but he couldn't help it. Walking into the office where Randy once again sat behind the desk that was situated in the middle of the room, Travis slid into one of the chairs across from the desk and stretched out his legs.

"I met the most amazing woman on the way home this afternoon."

Randy rolled his eyes and shook his head. "You must have found some poor woman having car trouble and offered her a ride back to town."

"Well, that's close, but take away the car and you're closer to the truth."

"Huh?" Randy's confused expression was priceless.

"She was huddled under a garbage bag on the side of the road. I thought when I stopped it would probably end up being a kitten or puppy that someone had put out. Instead, it was a person." Travis waited for what he'd just said to sink in. He wasn't disappointed.

"Someone put a woman out on the side of the road in a fucking garbage bag! Who in the hell would do something like that? Is she okay?" Randy had both hands flat on the desk as he stood up and leaned over it.

"Settle down. She's fine. Well, after I got her something to drink and eat. She hadn't had anything since yesterday when it happened. The poor thing has been walking all this time and slept in an abandoned car overnight."

"The hell you say. That's criminal. How could anyone do that to another human being?" Randy shook his head and eased back down in the chair. "Where is she now?"

"I took her to Helen's place. She wanted me to take her to a shelter, and Helen's is as close as we have here. She doesn't have to know it's really a boarding house for anyone in need."

"Good. Helen will take care of her." Randy ran a hand over his face.

"The good news is that she's got bookkeeping experience. I plan to offer her the job we have here after I check out this reference." Travis waved the piece of paper with Angela's old boss's name and phone number on it. "We can move her into the cabin so she will be close by. I would offer her a room in the house with us except I don't think she'd take it. Still, she has to be on the ranch in order to get to work each day. We can't go get her every day and take her back, and she doesn't have transportation."

Randy watched him the entire time he was talking without saying anything. Travis stared at him once he'd finished. Finally, after a few minutes of silence, his brother spoke up.

"I think you've taken a shine to her. I've never seen you so stirred up over a woman before." Randy leaned back in the chair and looked at him with a thoughtful expression. "What is her name?"

"Angela Carter. She's from Belzoni, Mississippi." He told his brother the entire story as she'd told it to him.

"Well, make that call and find out if she's someone we can take a chance on or not." Randy stood up and walked toward the door. "I'm going to check on how the hands are doing. You can fill me in at dinner tonight about what you've found out. I'll leave the particulars to you."

Travis watched his brother leave and wondered what that was all about. He would have thought the other man would be happy to find someone that could take some of the burden from their shoulders by handling the office. Not to mention that she was a pretty single woman that Travis found attractive and sexy as hell. Shaking it off, Travis moved to the other side of the desk and picked up the phone.

Twenty minutes later, he felt much better about Angela. The man on the other end of the phone had made it plain that he was disappointed in the young woman for leaving, but he hadn't had anything bad to say about her. She had done her job and was good at it. The man had wished him luck in keeping her though. He found that a little funny since she'd worked for the man for almost six years, from the time she had been sixteen until a couple of years after she graduated from the community college.

Standing up, he stretched and walked down the hall to the kitchen. It was his turn to fix dinner. Neither he nor his brother was an excellent cook, but they managed to make decent meals. Tonight he planned on something quick and easy. They had a lot to talk about and plans to make. He wanted to be sure the cabin was in good condition. They more or less kept it clean in case anyone in the family wanted to use it, but it probably needed airing out after the winter. It was supposed to be a pretty day tomorrow. They could leave the windows open all day.

The little cabin only had two rooms. The main room held a small living area with a tiny kitchen on the other side, complete with a table and chairs. The other one was a bedroom with the bathroom off of it. He felt like it would be plenty of room for her while she was getting on her feet. He hoped that things would work out and that she was the perfect woman for him and his brother to share. They had dreamed of a woman to love between them since they'd been old enough to understand the ménage lifestyle that their parents had lived.

He sighed. It would all depend on how she and Randy got along. He worried his brother would resist though. Lately, he had been less and less hopeful of finding someone they both could agree on and who would accept both of them in her life. They'd been stung several times in the past with Randy suffering the most. He didn't want that to happen again, but how did you find someone if you didn't step out and try?

By the time his brother had made it back in, Travis had everything ready. While Randy showered, he set the table and settled on how he would present everything to him. He couldn't explain it, but something deep in his heart said she was the one who could make their dreams come true. Now if only he could convince Randy to take a chance one more time.

Travis smiled when Randy walked back into the kitchen freshly showered. He squared his shoulders and offered him a beer.

Chapter Three

Angela checked her appearance in the bathroom mirror one more time. She didn't have makeup to fiddle with, so all she could really do was mess with her hair, and there was no taming it as she'd found out long ago. It hung down to her shoulders in ringlets. If she tried to brush it too much, they frizzed up. Her bangs could use a professional trimming, but she would keep taking care of them until she had some money saved before she wasted it on a haircut.

The Woods men would be along soon. Helen had taken a call from them after lunch that they would arrive at three to talk to Angela. She glanced over at the cheap windup clock on the bedside table as she returned to the bedroom. With less than five minutes left, she worried that she was getting her hopes up over the job possibility for nothing. After all, the only real job she'd had, she'd essentially walked away from after only giving a week's notice. She drew in a deep breath and let it out slowly to help calm her racing heart.

Stepping out of her temporary room, Angela closed the door and walked downstairs to wait in the office with Helen. Just as she knocked on the woman's open door, the front door opened and Travis walked in with another man right behind him who looked so much like him that he had to be his brother. She froze as Helen walked out beside her.

"Well, come on in, you two. It's always a pleasure for you to stop by. Go on into the front room and make yourselves at home." Helen ushered them into a common room of sorts that held a TV and a multitude of chairs and couches scattered around the room. "I'll run to get the coffee then leave you alone to talk."

Angela felt as if she had been thrown to the lions for some reason. She wasn't sure why she suddenly felt nervous and shy. She and Travis had gotten along fine the day before. She glanced around at the various places to sit and was relieved when Travis led them over to where two love seats sat across from each other with a coffee table between them. She sat down on one of them and they took the other.

"Angela, this is my brother, Randy." He indicated the other man sitting next to him.

He looked a lot like Travis except his hair was a shade lighter and his eyes were hazel instead of his brother's warm brown. He wasn't as tall as Travis either, but he had the same muscular build with a trim waist and juicy butt she would love to...

"This is Angela Carter." Travis's voice cut into her wayward thoughts.

She nodded her head at the other man and tried to school her features to be calm. It wouldn't help her cause if she appeared to be flighty and unorganized. She pasted a smile on as well.

"It's a pleasure to meet you." The other man held out his hand expectantly.

"Likewise, Ms. Carter." She allowed him to clasp her hand in his giant paw and nearly jerked it back when a spark ran up her arm from the brief contact.

Randy nodded but seemed a little distracted.

"Angela. Please call me Angela," she managed after an awkward second.

"Angela, then. Travis told me about how you ended up on the side of the road yesterday. I'm glad he found you. It can be real dangerous out there on your own like that."

She felt her smile drop a little. She wasn't quite sure Randy was as happy about it as he said he was. There was something in his voice that worried her. It wasn't that he scared her or even that he sounded disapproving. She didn't feel like he was a threat at all, but his expression seemed guarded, like he expected her to disappoint him somehow.

"I've talked with Randy about the job that we have taking care of the office on the ranch and he agrees that you would be perfect for it. Your employer in Belzoni was pleased with your work. He just wasn't very happy that you left so suddenly." Travis smiled across the coffee table at her. "We'd like to offer you the job with a three-month probation period where we see how you are able to handle the job. If at the end of that time you're doing well, we'd like to offer you a full-time position complete with a benefits package like the rest of our employees have." Travis quoted a salary to start her first three months that sounded quite fair to her.

She was just about to agree to the terms when he continued talking.

"Since you don't have transportation, you will need to live on the ranch where you can walk to and from work. There's a small cabin that you can use for as long as you wish. It's not much and is by no means fancy, but it's clean and sturdy and comes furnished."

She stared at him with wide eyes. This was far more than she would have ever believed. Why would they offer her a fair salary and a place to live without even really knowing her? It didn't make sense. Unease flitted at the edge of her thoughts that they might expect more from her than she was willing to give. Surely not. Travis had been so nice and careful around her.

"Well? What do you think, Angela?" Travis rubbed his hands up and down his thighs as if he was as nervous as she was.

"I–I don't know what to think. It's too generous. Surely you must want rent for the cabin."

"No rent. Too much trouble to deal with," Randy spoke up abruptly. "The office job can be stressful, so you'll more than earn your salary plus the rent."

She looked from Randy to Travis, trying to figure out their angle. Did they expect her to sleep with them for the job and place to live?

Again the thought of how Travis had been so nice to her soothed her worries. She needed the job and Travis was right. She didn't have any way to get to and from work. She would accept the position and if they turned out to be smarmy she could always quit.

"I really appreciate the chance at the job. I'll take it, and I promise to do my best."

Before she'd even finished talking, Travis jumped up and, leaning over the coffee table, grabbed her hand in his. He shook it, a giant smile on his face. When he let go, Randy stood up and did the same minus the giant smile. His was more reserved, but she wasn't going to let it bother her. Everyone was different, and more than likely Randy just wasn't as outgoing as his brother Travis seemed to be.

"Can you start on Monday? You can move in today so you can get comfortable with your new home. We can wait while you pack up and take you on back with us." Travis's enthusiasm boiled over, infecting her as well.

Suddenly she was anxious to start her new life. She didn't have much to pack, so it wouldn't take her more than fifteen minutes to gather it and to say good-bye to Helen.

"That would be fine. It will only take me a few minutes to pack." She stood up just as Helen walked in with coffee and cake.

"Goodness, have you already finished your meeting? Don't hurry away just yet." She let Randy take the tray from her hands then set about pouring coffee and cutting the small loaf.

"I'll run pack and then be right back down." Angela beamed at Helen before slipping from the room.

She hurried up the stairs to her room. She quickly packed up the clothes Helen had found for her in a small duffle bag she'd added to the pile as well. Angela was going to make sure that once she was on her feet she returned the favor with some donated clothes and funds. The shelter had been a godsend to her, as had Travis.

When she walked back into the front room, the men were sipping coffee and listening to Helen talk about the latest gossip around town.

Both men stood up when she entered the room. She wasn't used to such manners. While Mississippi was known for being the hospitality state, she had never warranted special behavior before. If she wasn't careful, it would turn her head. She didn't need to start anything with her new bosses. That was a sure way to lose the best thing that had happened to her in a long time.

"Are you ready?" Randy asked.

"Let her sit and have some coffee and a piece of this delicious cake Helen made, Randy." Travis shoved his brother with his shoulder.

Both men returned to their seats once she had settled back on the couch across from them. Helen handed her a plate with a piece of the wonderful-smelling cake. She could tell that Randy was ready to go, so she ate quickly, not wanting to hold him up.

"Helen, I can't thank you enough for all you've done for me," she began.

"Nonsense. You've barely been here a full day. I'm going to miss having you around. I don't get many women to talk to here. Be sure and come see me when you're in town for anything. We'll have a nice visit." Helen took her hand as they stood up.

"I'll carry this to the kitchen for you." Travis picked up the tray with their cups and saucers and followed the kind woman into the kitchen, leaving Angela alone with Randy.

Tension stretched between them as Travis seemed to be taking his time returning. She felt as if she should say something, but nothing came to mind. She didn't know Randy well enough to make small talk. His eyes remained on her the entire time they waited, making Angela uncomfortable. She was just about to say something about it when Travis finally emerged from the back.

"Ready?" he asked, oblivious to the stress focused between Angela and Randy.

"Yes," she quickly answered then wished she could take it back. She had sounded so pathetic.

Travis looked from Randy over to her and then back at Randy but didn't comment. Maybe he wasn't as immune to the tension as she'd first thought. Without commenting, he took her small satchel and led the way toward the door.

* * * *

Randy wanted to kick himself for acting so unfriendly. It wasn't that he didn't like her, because he did—so far. It was that Travis was already smitten with her. They had no idea if she could do the job or not, and he had a feeling that Travis wanted her to be more than just an office manager and bookkeeper for them. From the way he was acting, Randy was almost positive that he saw her as a potential girlfriend for both of them. He wasn't about to get caught in that mess again. His brother might still be looking for that elusive woman to be their shared wife, but Randy had already given up on that pipe dream.

Just because their parents had found each other and everything had worked out didn't mean that it would for them. It was time to grow up and realize that the real world just didn't work that way. Sure, there were a few ménage relationships in Riverbend, but he couldn't see it working for them.

The last time they'd tried that route, Belinda, their girlfriend, had just about put them both in the ground. She had planned to marry one of them, sure, but not both of them. She didn't want a permanent ménage relationship. She thought she could choose one over the other with the losing brother backing away. What had been so bad about it was that both he and Travis had fallen for her. She'd never once let on that she wasn't completely on board with their plans. They had been honest with her up front, but she had foolishly thought she could convince the one she had chosen to follow her plans instead. The fact that she'd chosen Randy had almost caused a rift between them that wouldn't heal.

No, he wanted no part of another *ménage marriage* attempt. He would be sure and stress that to his brother the first chance he got. The fact that they had talked about her the night before wasn't lost on Randy. Travis hadn't bothered to say anything about his ulterior motive. Or had he? Maybe there had been some hints that he just hadn't picked up on. Maybe he hadn't wanted to pick up on them.

Randy rubbed his hands over his face before climbing into the cab of his truck. He closed the door, waiting on Travis to stow Angela's bag in the backseat before helping her into the front. He noted with a smile that she had expected to ride in the back with her bag. Yeah, Travis was knee deep in plans that Randy intended to put a stop to.

"Randy, head on over to the grocery store," his brother said as he climbed up to sit next to Angela. "She's going to need groceries to get her through until she gets her first paycheck."

Nodding, he waited for them both to get settled and buckled in before he backed out of the parking spot and turned toward the other side of town.

"Um, I'll pay you back with my first check or you can just deduct it. I appreciate the loan." She frowned as she clasped her hands together in a tight grasp.

"Got to eat to work," he said in a gruff voice.

Travis glared at him, but Angela seemed oblivious to the tension in the truck. He hadn't meant it to come out sounding so sarcastic. What the hell was wrong with him? He liked her even though he didn't know her very well. Why did everything that came out of his mouth around her sound like an insult?

He pulled into a parking spot in front of the store. When they walked inside, Angela grabbed a buggy. Travis grabbed his arm and stopped him from following her.

"What the fuck is your problem? I thought you agreed on giving her a try?"

"I did. I do, but you're treating her more like a girlfriend, and we don't know anything about her really. What's up with that?"

His brother sighed and let his head drop back for a second. Randy had been right. Travis did fancy her as a possible girlfriend for them. He had never known his brother to jump into something so fast before.

"She's different, Randy. Give her a chance. There's just something about her that I can't describe." Travis hurried to catch up with Angela, who'd moved ahead of them.

Randy followed a few steps behind and watched them. Her shining red hair nearly glowed under the florescent lights in the store. It hung down her back in gentle ringlets. She moved with the grace of a dancer, though she was barely tall enough to come to his chin. He couldn't help but notice her well-rounded ass or the curve of her breasts. He was sure they would fit comfortably in his hands.

He almost stumbled as he realized that he was thinking about her as a woman and not as their new employee. He needed to stop that right now. He lengthened his stride to catch up with them and forced himself to relax. She shopped quickly, seeming to know what she wanted without needing to browse to make up her mind. He liked that.

Something else he noticed was that she didn't buy a lot either. In fact, she hadn't really bought enough to keep her healthy. He frowned as he took in the contents of her basket, ramen noodles, cheese, crackers, bread, peanut butter, and juice. He looked over at Travis. He was frowning as well. She was buying cheap stuff as if she didn't expect to be able to buy decent food in the first place.

"Angela. Why are you picking out all that crap? You can't live on that stuff," he said with a frown.

She looked up at him and smiled. It lit up her face and the sparkle in those bright blue eyes nearly sent him to his knees.

"It's what I always eat. I like it fine."

"Well that stops now. You need healthy food if you're going to be working for us. Do you know how to cook?"

She frowned at him and lifted her chin. "I'm a good cook. My momma taught me how from the time I could stand on a chair and help her."

"Good. Let's start over. Travis, go and get another buggy and we'll leave this one here." Randy took Angela's hand without thinking about it and headed back across the store to the produce section.

"Hey! Wait a minute. What is going on?" Angela pulled at her hand when they stopped in front of the fresh vegetables.

"Angela, you've been eating like a starving college student. You can afford to eat things you like and that are good for you." Randy looked over her head impatiently for Travis to hurry up.

When he looked back down, he could tell he'd hurt her feelings, her mouth tight in a stubborn line. Hell, he hadn't meant to insult her. He just didn't like the idea that she hadn't been able to eat good food. He sighed and was relieved when Travis joined, them pushing an empty cart. Travis looked from Angela to him and his scowl grew deeper before he changed it to an easy smile for Angela.

"Let's pick out something else. Hey. Maybe you could cook for us one night. Neither one of us can cook worth a damn," Travis said.

Randy watched her expression lighten at the thought. He wished he'd been the one to put the smile on her face since he'd been the one to make her frown. He decided to try and keep his mouth shut for now. It could only be an improvement where she was concerned.

"I'd love to cook something for you. I owe you both so much for helping me and taking a chance on me like this."

"You don't owe us anything. You're the one who is going to be helping us out of a mess. We've needed an office manager and bookkeeper for a long time now. Wait until you see the mess we've made of things."

Randy followed along behind them as they picked out fresh fruit and vegetables. It was obvious that she knew how to choose them by the way she picked them up and smelled or squeezed them. She actually appeared to be picky. When they moved on to the meats, she was just as choosey. Since they raised cattle, they did know how to pick out meat, so he was impressed with her choices. He felt even more like a fool.

After checking out, he and Travis loaded the groceries into the backseat of the truck while Angela climbed into the front. Once they were all buckled in, he pulled out of the parking lot and started home. Travis and Angela chatted like old friends the entire way. He couldn't help but feel a little jealous at their easy way with each other. He felt left out, but it was his own damn fault. Travis had been right, she was special. He'd been too caught up in making sure his brother wasn't getting them into something he was sure would never work to notice at first.

As they turned onto the road leading to their house, they drove under the sign announcing their ranch, Wood's Wilderness. Their brand was two intertwined *W*'s and it was displayed on the sign. Angela gasped at the sight.

"Wow! I guess I didn't realize how big this would be. You have your own road and sign and everything."

"We'll take you on a tour one day soon. We've slowly added to it since we bought the original spread. It's one of the larger ranches in the area. Jared and Quade own a larger one on the other side of town," Travis told her.

"I can't wait to get started in the office." Angela's face beamed with excitement.

Randy smiled at her enthusiasm. He couldn't help but be affected by it. He hoped once she saw the mess they had that she wouldn't turn and hightail it out of there.

"Well, Monday will be soon enough. You need time to get settled into the cabin and rest up after everything you've been through." Randy spoke up before he realized it.

"Oh, but that's three days away. Are you sure you don't want me to start tomorrow?" She turned to look at him as he pulled up in front of the little cabin she would be living in.

"I'm sure. It's waited this long, another few days won't hurt." Travis backed him up.

They climbed out of the truck. Travis helped Angela down. He grabbed two bags of groceries while Travis got the other two. When Angela started to grab her things, Travis told her to leave them for now.

"We'll come back out and get them. Come see if this will be okay for you." He led her up the steps to the little porch and juggled the bags to open the door.

When Randy followed them inside, it was to hear Angela gasp in obvious pleasure. By the smile on her face, she was more than happy with it. He couldn't take his eyes off of how her bright blue eyes sparkled.

"It's lovely! I never would have imagined anything this nice when you said it was just a little cabin." She followed them across the room to the tiny kitchen where they set their bags down on the short counter and the small bar area that separated the kitchen from the rest of the cabin.

"Why don't you put away the groceries so you'll know where everything is? I'm going out to get your things." Travis gave Randy a hard stare before he walked back out the door.

He knew his brother was warning him to be on his best behavior. He had every intention of doing that. He'd screwed up and wasn't planning on doing it again.

"There isn't a dishwasher, but the microwave and fridge are brand new. The stove has barely been used. I hope you're okay with gas." Randy watched her as she explored the kitchen as she started putting away the food.

"Oh, there's no need for a dishwasher for just one person. This is all so nice and clean. I can't wait to cook something."

The door opened and Travis walked back in carrying her duffle bag and set it on the couch before walking over to where Randy stood propped against the bar.

"As soon as you finish that, we'll show you around the cabin," his brother said.

She nodded and quickly finished what she was doing, storing the empty bags as well. After giving the kitchen one more glance, she indicated she was ready to look around. Travis retrieved her things and led the way to the bedroom in the back.

"Oh, my goodness! This is perfect!" Angela put her hand to her mouth as she took in the room around her.

The bedroom was almost as big as the front part of the house with a queen-size bed and matching chest and dresser. The headboard had been their mom's from when she'd been a little girl and was hand carved. There was a small chair off to one side with a lamp and table that he knew would be a perfect spot to sit and read. She opened one of the two doors and cooed over the large walk-in closet then checked the next door and gasped at the very modern bathroom complete with whirlpool tub and separate walk-in shower. When the previous owners had built the cabin, it had been for their wife's sister to give her some privacy. Once he and his brother had bought the ranch it had only been used as a guest house when their family visited on occasion.

"This is so nice. I never would have imagined anything like this." Angela turned away from them and walked over to the window.

Randy wasn't fooled. He'd seen the sheen of tears in her eyes. Why would she cry about a two-room cabin? He looked over at his brother. He looked as baffled as Randy felt. When she turned back around she had regained her composure and was smiling.

"Thanks so much for letting me stay here. It's perfect. Are you sure I can't start work tomorrow? I want to get busy."

"We had much rather you rest and settle in and start fresh on Monday. Besides." Travis grinned at her. "You promised to cook for us, remember? You can do that tomorrow night, after you've rested up some."

Randy had to swallow hard when she literally beamed at them. It gave her entire face an angelic glow that suited her name. How could anyone have put her out on the side of the road? He wished he could have just five minutes alone with the bastard. Just like that, it hit him. He was already a little in love with their Angela. How the hell had that happened so fast?

Chapter Four

Angela rushed through her shower, nerves sending dolphins splashing around in her stomach. Why was she letting a simple dinner get her so upset? Sure, they were her new bosses, but they weren't hiring her on the basis of how well she could cook. As soon as she had dried off, she pulled on a pair of jeans and one of the blouses from the shelter. It looked brand new, and the deep blue color looked nice on her.

The clock on the bedside table indicated she had fifteen minutes before they would arrive. There would be plenty of time to finish setting the table and check everything. She wanted everything to be perfect. They were like her fairy godmothers or something. The least she could do to thank them was cook them a good home-cooked meal and do her best at the job.

No sooner had she filled the glasses with ice than there was a knock at the door. Angela glanced around to be sure she hadn't forgotten something before hurrying over to the door. She swallowed around the knot in her throat and drew in a deep breath before opening the door.

The first thing she saw when she opened the door was a bouquet of wild flowers hiding the faces of the two men standing at the door. Stunned, she didn't say anything for several seconds until the sound of one of the men clearing their throats caught her attention.

"Oh, my goodness. Come in. I–I was startled by the flowers. They're beautiful." She stepped aside to let them in.

"Thought they would help brighten the room up for you." Travis took the vase of flowers from Randy's hands and set it on the table in the open living area. "Hope you're not allergic or anything."

Angela shook her head *no* when she noticed Randy frown at his brother's statement.

"No. I'm not allergic to anything that I know of. I've got dinner ready. Would you like tea or water?"

Randy smiled again. "Tea would be great."

"I'll have tea, too," Travis said.

She pulled the pitcher from the fridge and poured three glasses full. Before she could grab them, Travis carried all three of them to the table. When she turned around to see about the food, Randy stood right behind her.

"Need help with the food? That"—he indicated the platter with the roast and potatoes—"looks heavy."

"Um, yes, thank you." She picked up the bowl with the peas in one hand and the bowl of rice in the other.

Once everything was on the table, she sat and waited for them to dig in. Instead, they stared at her. What had she forgotten? She started to panic.

"You first, Angela," Travis finally said.

"Oh, goodness. You didn't have to wait on me." She quickly picked up the peas and after spooning some onto her plate, passed it around.

They quickly filled their plates, and when Randy and Travis started eating, Angela breathed a sigh of relief. It must be okay since they were plowing through it so fast.

"This has got to be the best home-cooked meal I've had since the last time mom and the dads were here," Randy said.

"Um, dads? I don't understand." She frowned.

"Our mom is married to two men. We have two fathers," Travis explained. "Ménage relationships are not unusual around River Bend."

"Oh." She really didn't know what to say to that.

The men continued to talk about her cooking ability as she tried to comprehend the unorthodox relationship they seemed to accept as normal. Angela scolded herself for not paying attention to what the brothers were talking about. She should be paying attention to them.

"I don't think I've ever had anything this good before," Randy was saying.

"You're not kidding. I think we hired her for the wrong thing." Travis reached over and squeezed her arm before he went back to eating.

Angela felt her heart lighten at the praise. No one had ever really complimented her on anything before. Well, outside of her mom. It felt good to hear it. She just prayed she would be able to do as well with the job she was hired for when the time came. She had never really worried about being able to do her job back home, but she had no idea what to expect on a ranch. There were bound to be things she didn't know anything about.

"What are you frowning for, Angel?" Travis asked.

"Angel?" Angela smiled.

"You're pretty as an angel and cook like one, too," he said. "Do you mind if I call you Angel?"

"No, I don't mind. No one's ever shortened my name before." She could feel a blush warming her neck and cheeks.

"Let's get these dishes washed so we can sit out on the porch and enjoy the sunset." Randy stood up and began gathering the dirty plates and silverware.

"Oh, goodness. You don't have to help. I'll get them later. You're my guests." Angela rushed to take them from his hands.

Randy chuckled and held them over her head. "Of course we're going to help. We asked you to cook for us. I'm not leaving you with a ton of dirty dishes to wash up."

Travis had grabbed some bowls and was right behind his brother. With nowhere to go but farther into the kitchen area, Angela ran water in the sink and added soap. She supposed they would be doing the dishes after all. Travis hip bumped her out of the way and began washing while his brother dried. When Randy handed her a dry plate, she put it away with a sigh. Despite the area being small, they somehow managed to all fit in and get the dishes washed and put away without breaking anything or stepping on anyone's toes, though there were several hip bumps here and there.

"See. That didn't take long at all with all three of us doing them." Travis ushered her toward the door. "Now we have time to sit on the porch and watch the sunset."

"Um, guys. I don't have any chairs on the porch to sit in," she said.

"Oh, we're going to walk over to ours. Besides, you can see more up there than down here." Randy took her hand and dragged her through the door and down the steps.

When he didn't let go, Angela resigned herself to being carried along as they walked toward the main house that sat up a small rise about a hundred and fifty yards away. As soon as they stepped up on the porch, Randy steered her to the middle rocking chair.

"What would you like to drink, Angel?" Travis asked.

"Oh, nothing right now, thanks." She settled back and let herself relax as the men claimed chairs on either side of her.

"I think this is my favorite part of the day," Randy said. "Sitting here after dinner, watching the sky darken as the sun sets."

"Watching the sun rise with a steaming cup of coffee is nice, too," Travis added.

"Do you do this every night?" Angela couldn't imagine being able to enjoy this view all the time.

Back home there had always been something that needed doing and even when she had some spare time, there wasn't a view like this to enjoy. They had lived close to the catfish ponds, and the bugs were terrible there. Just the idea that it was available when she had time was awesome. She could easily get used to seeing the way the blue sky changed colors as the sun dipped low over the horizon.

"We do every chance we get. During calving season we're pretty busy, but we manage to catch the show at least once or twice a week regardless," Randy answered.

They all remained silent while the sun slowly sank from the sky. The beauty of it seemed to add peace to her soul. Angela wanted to sit there forever and bask in the quiet wonder of being alive. Unfortunately, this wasn't her home and she was their employee, not their girlfriend. She needed to remember that and stop noticing how good they filled out their jeans or how tantalizing it was to watch their muscles ripple beneath the material of their shirts.

With a soft sigh, she stood up and stretched. It was time she returned to her little cabin and got ready for bed. She wanted to get plenty of rest and be ready come Monday to start her new job.

"I really enjoyed the sunset, guys, but I need to head back to the cabin." She started across the porch but Randy stopped her with a hand on her arm.

"What's the rush? Tomorrow's Sunday. You can sleep in and relax tomorrow."

"Besides, we wanted to get to know you a little better, Angel." Travis stood up as well.

Angela looked up at both of them, her mouth suddenly dry as she noticed how their voices had deepened. She tried to swallow and ended up coughing instead.

"Come on inside. We'll get you something to drink." Travis walked across the porch and opened the door, leaving his brother to usher her inside.

She reached up and took Randy's outstretched hand and let him pull her to her feet. He smiled down at her before running his hand down her arm and over to her lower back, where he rested it as he ushered her inside their home.

The entrance had a homey feel right away. A coat rack on the wall next to the door held plenty of room for lots of coats with a place to take off your boots beneath it. The rich hardwood floors were clean but not polished. She could easily imagine how they would look with a nice shine to them. Randy urged her left, where the room opened up into a roomy living area complete with a stone fireplace and massive wall-mounted TV. The chairs and couches all looked like real leather that they obviously used on a regular basis.

A small entryway separated the living area from the large eat-in kitchen. As she stepped into the room, a feeling of home enveloped her. Though the design screamed out old-time farm kitchen, it had been totally updated with state-of-the-art appliances complete with a massive industrial-sized refrigerator. Angela couldn't even imagine how you would ever fill it up. The beautiful marble-topped counters and generous cabinets had her itching to explore. A four-person bar separated the kitchen proper from the eat-in breakfast area where a table large enough to seat at least eight people sat in the center of the room.

"Wow! You've got a really nice house. I love the kitchen." Angela wanted to slap her hand over her mouth at how country that sounded.

"Thanks. We haven't really done anything to the place since we bought it several years ago. It needs some work." Travis had pulled three glasses down from the cabinets. "What would like to drink? We've got iced tea, lemonade, water, and beer."

"Oh, um, lemonade sounds good."

Randy led her over to the bar and helped her climb up on one of the comfortable bar stools. His hand left her back to rest along the top of her stool. Somehow she could still feel the heat of it against her skin. A small shiver raced down her spine as she took a sip of the lemonade Travis set in front of her.

"Mmm, this is good."

"Lemonade and tea are about the only things our momma managed to teach us that tastes decent every time," Travis said with a chuckle.

"Yeah, I'm thinking maybe we should hire Angela to be our cook instead of wasting her on office work." Randy looked serious when she glanced his way.

"Naw, I think we'll keep her in the office and maybe she'll take pity on us and cook us a meal once in a while." Travis grinned at her as he leaned on the counter across from her.

"I'll cook for you anytime you want me to. I don't mind one bit. Cooking is easy."

"Not for us it isn't. We tend to burn most things we cook." Randy sipped on his lemonade.

"Ain't that the truth, brother?" Travis tapped his glass against Randy's before taking a swallow. "How do you like the cabin? Do you need anything?"

"I love it! It's perfect for me." She couldn't help but grin at the thought of the lovely little cabin.

"Good. We want you to be comfortable and enjoy your downtime. You're going to find out that the office can be real stressful at times." Randy frowned when she looked at him.

"Randy isn't kidding, Angel. That's why we're so happy that you're going to take it off our shoulders." Travis smiled, his warm chocolate eyes capturing hers with their beauty.

The ringing of one of their cell phones jerked her back to awareness. She couldn't believe she'd zoned out like that just looking into Travis's eyes. She had to get hold of herself if she was going to be working for the two men. She couldn't screw up this opportunity by getting romantic feelings for her bosses. She cast a quick look in Randy's direction as he answered his phone. Even though he'd been a little cool toward her at first, he'd relaxed some now.

"Hell. Yeah, we'll be out there in a few minutes." Randy stuffed the phone back in the holster attached to his belt with a sigh.

"What is it?" Travis asked.

"Couple of cows got tangled up in the barbed wire fencing somehow. Nothing deep enough for actual stitches, but there are a lot of cuts and the fence is down."

"I better head back to my place so you can go. Thanks for the lemonade." Angela quickly turned on the stool and tried to jump down.

Much to her embarrassment, she misjudged how far the floor was from where she was sitting and nearly fell. Randy quickly pulled her into his arms to keep her from falling.

"Whoa there, honey. No need to get in that big of a hurry. The guys have it under control. We'll walk you back to the cabin. It's dark and you don't know your way yet." He didn't immediately release her from his arms. She shivered.

When she looked up, it was to see Randy's intense hazel eyes peering down at her with a puzzled expression on his face. Before she could ask what was wrong, he stepped back, dropping his arms in the process. He indicated with a nod of his head that she was to lead the way back to the front door. She could feel him at her back as she walked through the living area into the entrance hall. Travis reached around her and opened the front door.

When they reached her tiny front porch, Angela turned to thank them for walking her back. Before she managed to open her mouth, Randy bent down and rested his lips against her forehead for a brief second. Then he stepped back and Travis did the same thing.

"Goodnight, Angel. Have a good night and get plenty of rest tomorrow. Monday morning starts at seven."

She just nodded her head as they turned and disappeared into the night. After a few seconds, Angela shook her head in bewilderment before going inside and closing the door. She couldn't help but wonder what she had gotten herself into. Like she'd learned over and over again, sometimes things were too good to be true. As much as she didn't want that to be the case with her current situation, Angela wasn't a fool and hadn't been born yesterday. Travis and Randy expected her to be their office manager with fringe benefits. Despite how mouthwateringly delicious they looked, the day she couldn't resist them was the day she would hand in her notice and leave. Nothing lasted forever. After all, her life was a testament to that.

Chapter Five

Monday morning Angela walked up to the ranch house where she was to meet Travis and Randy at seven. She stepped up on the porch with butterflies flitting around in her stomach. She had been up since five that morning, trying to prepare herself for whatever was to come and praying that everything would be fine despite her worries that the guys expected more than she was willing to give. With a final sigh, she knocked on the door and waited.

She heard booted heels crossing the floor before the door opened. Randy grinned and stepped back.

"You don't have to knock on the door. You can come and go as you please. The office is right this way."

He led her to the right where a door opened into a large room with several file cabinets and a large oak desk with a matching credenza behind it under a picture window. Two comfortable-looking chairs stood in front of the desk. She stopped beside the desk to wait for Randy to tell her where she needed to start.

"I think the first thing that needs doing is figuring out where we stand on paying bills. When I work in the office, I pay whatever comes in while I'm here, but I'm not sure what comes in and doesn't get looked at between times. Travis will go through and pay the old stuff and leave the new stuff for later."

"That could leave something to slip through the cracks and not get paid on time." Angela nodded her head. "Okay. I'll start with organizing the desk and locating all the bills. Do you write checks on the computer or by hand and what about record keeping? Where do you record your entries?"

Randy walked over to the computer on the desk and logged in. Then he pulled up a program that looked like it was made for ranching from what she could see of it. She hoped it wouldn't be difficult to figure out.

"We'll set you up with a password and then you can log in. It's a very comprehensive program that has different uses all over the ranch. I'll slowly show them all to you over time, but for now, you can concentrate on the overall bookkeeping part of it for us."

He pulled back the office chair and waited until she'd taken a seat before he started again. "Okay, I've set your username as your name. All you have to do is choose a password when you get ready to. For now, let's look over the program."

For the next two hours, Angela sat while Randy stood over her, explaining how the program worked and what they normally did on a day-to-day basis. The phone rang off and on, but Randy ignored it, letting someone else pick it up since it rarely rang more than three times in a row.

A little after nine, his cell phone rang and he stepped across the room to talk to someone on the other end while Angela continued exploring in the computer. She felt like she had a pretty good grasp of how it worked and what they were doing as far as paying bills and the few payments that came in when they sold cattle. They also had a rather impressive stock portfolio that was managed by an outside broker. All Angela had to do was keep up with any dividends that paid out and move the numbers around when they made changes to the portfolio for some reason. She had never dealt with the amount of money that changed hands in the ranching business before. The store back in Belzoni had been small with a modest bottom line at best. This was almost overwhelming to her. Nervousness that she'd bitten off more than she could chew had almost led her to tell Randy she couldn't do the job, but he kept assuring her she was doing fine.

She picked up the pad she had been making notes on and skimmed through it as Randy continued to argue with someone about a horse. She could tell he was aggravated, but he didn't raise his voice or curse the entire time he was on the phone. She couldn't help but wonder what was wrong. She heard him tell whoever was on the phone that he wasn't interested before he disconnected.

"Sorry." He walked back over to stand next to her. "So, do you think you've got a handle on that part?"

"I think so. Basically it's like most accounting packages with some added bells and whistles to keep track of which cows you sell and which ones you buy. I can always ask if I have a question, right?"

"Right. How about some coffee before Travis shows up to go over the breeding entries and such?" Randy grinned down at her.

Angela struggled to keep the shock from showing on her face as she stood up. Breeding entries? What was she supposed to do with those? Giant butterflies resumed their winged flight inside her belly. She didn't know the first thing about breeding cows.

"I've been dealing with most of the cash flow side of the ranch and Travis has been handling the paperwork and logistics for the actual running of the ranch like ordering supplies and keeping up with bloodlines. He'll go over that part with you."

They were drinking coffee at the bar, discussing how often they paid their accounts at various stores when Travis strolled in from a door off the kitchen. She gathered it led into a sort of mudroom since he wasn't wearing his boots or jacket when he walked in. His weary expression seemed to brighten as soon as he saw her sitting with his brother. It sent a little thrill through her to know that he was happy to see her there. Once again worry nibbled at her insides.

"Hey there, Angel. How has your morning been so far?"

"Hi, Travis. Good. Randy made the program seem easy. Let's just hope I absorbed enough to muddle through it when he's not around," she said.

"Don't listen to her. She took excellent notes that I don't even think she's going to need." Randy grinned over at her.

Travis poured a cup of coffee and eased onto the empty stool next to her. She couldn't help but be aware that she was sitting between two very handsome, very virile men. They seemed to ooze testosterone and sexiness from their pores. The thought of losing herself between them nearly had her falling off the stool.

"I better get out there and get some work done," Randy said. "I'll see you around noon, honey. Travis will take good care of you. Just don't let him get started on his favorite topic of breeding programs when he starts on the breeding part of the package or you'll never get anywhere. He's sort of obsessed with it." Randy winked at her as he walked off.

"Don't listen to him. Keeping good breeding records means the difference between quality beef and sick cows. Come on. Let's take this into the office." He stood up and waited on her to get down as well.

She followed him back into the office and settled back in the chair as Travis leaned over her to bring up the breeding program. The scent of horses, fresh air, and male musk filled her, making it difficult for her to concentrate on what he was saying at first. Angela struggled to ignore how good he smelled. It played havoc with her emotions since she'd had a similar reaction to his brother not an hour before. Guilt laced with discomfort edged out her anxiety about mastering the breeding program.

Angela took copious notes as Travis went over everything. He was actually an excellent instructor. He reviewed what he had already gone over before moving on to something new, giving her a chance to be sure she'd made notes on each step. When they had completed the program, he stepped back and grabbed a folder from the filing cabinet.

"This is last year's entries. Why don't you look through them and familiarize yourself with what the final result is, and I think you'll have it down just fine. Remember, I'll be giving you the information when we actually start the process and then the results and progress as things go along."

"I never knew there was so much that went into raising cows." She shook her head as she studied her notes. "I mean, I just thought you gave them food and water and sold them once they grew up."

Travis chuckled. "It's a little more complicated than that. If we didn't make sure to watch the breeding, we could end up with too much inbreeding, which leads to increased miscarriages and stillborn calves, not to mention all the health issues that come up. That means keeping up with their inoculation records as well."

"Okay. I have a lot to learn about this side of the business. What else do I need to know how to do?"

"Let's go over ordering supplies and how we handle that. We actually keep an inventory of what we have on hand and log in what we use or receive each day. That way, figuring out what we need to buy every week or month isn't as big of an issue. We can look at what we've been ordering and decide if that will work for the next order."

Angela nodded. "It would help to decide from one year to the next what you might need in the future as well. Like when you normally need more feed because of cold weather. I get it. That's really pretty smart. I never would have thought an inventory system would work for a ranch. I mean, who keeps up with how many bales of hay they have stacked somewhere?" She smiled and continued to read over her notes.

By the time noon had arrived, Angela felt as if she had a pretty good idea of how things worked and what her job would consist of on a daily basis. Besides the computer programs and the filing system, she also learned how to work the radio to locate various ranch hands and was given a cell phone for the ranch with everyone's number programed into it. That way she could reach anyone she might need unless they were in the extreme north or northwest area of the ranch. There all of the signals were weak.

"Come on, Angel, lunch time. We're in charge of making sandwiches today. Do you want to be in charge of the condiments or the meat?" Travis asked.

"I'll handle the meat. I don't know what you like on your sandwiches yet, but I can add the meat I think."

Travis quickly washed his hands when they reached the kitchen and while she did the same, he pulled out all the fixings for ham sandwiches. They quickly got into a rhythm and had eight sandwiches ready by the time Randy walked in thirty minutes later.

They ate at the table with a pitcher of tea and the plate of sandwiches along with a bucket of store-bought potato salad. Angela made a mental note to make them a batch of homemade potato salad when that ran out. It would taste a lot better in her opinion and wouldn't take long to whip up. Once the men had finished eating, there were three sandwiches left over. They wrapped them up for an afternoon snack.

"Okay, Angela. You have our cell phone numbers and the radio if you need anything. As far as the phone goes, just take a message unless it's family or an emergency of some kind." Travis walked with her back into the office.

"I think I have it. What time do you normally come back to the house in the afternoons?" she asked.

"You're finished at four, Angel. Don't wait around on us. We might be in by then or it might be closer to five or so before we finish."

"Okay. Do I lock anything up when I leave?"

"Nope. No need to around here. Just log off the computer before you go."

When she nodded and started to walk around the desk to sit down, Travis surprised her when he pulled her into a quick hug.

"You have no idea how glad we are to have you here, Angel. Hope the work doesn't run you off." He let her go and walked out of the office before she could form a coherent reply.

Damn, they were going to drive her crazy. She sank down onto the office chair and stared at the screen saver of a newborn calf for several minutes before she snapped out of it. It would probably take her all afternoon just to get the paperwork sorted into stacks that made sense. She needed to get started, especially if she planned to start dinner for the men. Even though she knew it was asking for trouble, Angela couldn't help but feel sorry for their lack of cooking skills.

By the time four o'clock rolled around, she had everything sorted and ready to work on the next morning. She was relieved to find that none of the bills were past due, but there were two that would be if she didn't get checks signed either that night or the next day. She would need to ask if they planned to hand deliver any of them or mail them all.

After making sure to log off the computer and secure all the stacks so that they wouldn't accidently get knocked off the desk, Angela hurried into the kitchen to wash her hands. She quickly explored the freezer, fridge, and large walk-in pantry she had located to figure out what her options were. She settled on meatloaf with creamed potatoes and peas. It would be a good meal that would probably leave enough leftover meatloaf for sandwiches the next day for lunch.

By the time the men stomped in the back door, Angela had the meatloaf in the oven and the potatoes boiling. She worried they would be upset that she'd made herself at home in their kitchen. Instead of being angry, they just stood there with their eyes closed, inhaling the scents of cooking as if it were the best smell in the world.

"As much as I can't wait for dinner to be ready, you shouldn't have cooked, honey," Randy said. "You've already put in a full day's job in the office."

"Shut up, Randy. I'll make sure we pay her for the overtime. It smells like heaven." Travis walked over to peek in the stove.

Angela popped him with the dish towel before she thought about it. "Don't do that, you change the oven temperature when you open the door."

He grinned when it dawned on her she'd just popped one of her bosses with a towel. Travis stalked toward her in long strides. Angela backed up until she was flush against the wall.

"Randy?" She looked over Travis's shoulder at his brother. "What's he going to do?"

"Don't know, honey. Guess you're going to have to ask him yourself."

"I'll tell you what I'm going to do, Angel. I'm going to turn you over my knee for popping me with that towel." The serious expression on his face didn't ring true with the amusement she saw in his eyes though.

"Now, Travis. I didn't mean anything by it. I just reacted like I did when I cooked back home."

"Maybe you should cut her some slack, brother. It's obvious she's sorry for doing it." Randy had moved to stand next to Travis.

"What do you suggest instead? I can't let her get away with it. If I do this time, what's to say next time she won't do something else like pinch me on the ass?"

"Well, you do have a point there." Randy leaned closer as Angela tried to control her breathing.

What where they doing to her? She felt as if her heart was going to pound right out of her chest. She resisted the urge to close her eyes. Instead, she lifted her chin and tried to act as if she wasn't the least bit affected by their teasing and close proximity. In truth, she'd never been as aware of a man in her life as she was now, boxed in by these two cowboys.

Travis's eyes flashed when her chin went up. Both men edged closer. She immediately pressed her hands against their chests in an effort to stop them. All it did was make her even more aware of their hard, sculpted chests and the heat that radiated from them. They both leaned in toward her, their eyes darkening in passion. Angela couldn't stop her body's reaction to their nearness. Her pussy dampened with need.

Hot, wet lips pressed against her cheeks from each side as they rested a hand on either side of her waist and pulled her toward them. All rational thought flew from her mind as female hormones took over so that she leaned into them. For a few brief seconds, all reason left her and all she could do was feel. Then reality snapped her back into the present with the dinging of the timer that the potatoes were ready. She jerked back against the wall even as she pushed at their chests to make them back away. Shame flooded her as heat raced up her neck to flash across her face.

"I'm not sleeping with you just because you gave me a job."

Chapter Six

Travis's jaw dropped as he took a step back. Things had gotten out of hand. They were moving way too fast and pushing her. He closed his mouth and tried to rein in his desire that threatened to ruin everything. He knew without a doubt that she was the one for them, but they had to get her on the same page before they scared her away.

"Angela, we're sorry. We didn't mean to make you feel uncomfortable." Randy had stepped back as well and had his hands out by his sides. "I think something is ready over there on the stove. Let's start over, and we promise to back off, okay?"

Travis watched as she bit her bottom lip and nodded. She didn't look scared as much as upset. They'd threatened her sense of self-worth by coming on to her like they had. If she thought the only reason they had hired her was to get her in their bed, they were in serious trouble. He could kick himself for letting things get out of hand. He knew better than to pressure someone. Neither he nor Randy would ever do that. What had he been thinking?

I wasn't thinking. That's the whole damn problem. I know she's right for us, and I just want to get to the good part of holding her and making her happy.

He watched as Randy walked back over to the stove and cut off the potatoes that were boiling. He stepped to one side and let Angela slip between him and the bar. He couldn't help but inhale the sweet scent of her that must have been a combination of her shampoo and something fresh and clean smelling even after a long day working in the office.

When she reached the stove, Angela reset the clock and started buttering rolls. He didn't pick up any further nervousness from her, so he relaxed and nodded at his brother who had positioned himself on the other side of the bar with a beer. Travis grabbed one for himself out of the fridge and leaned against the cabinet next to the doorway leading into the laundry room. It was actually a laundry and mud room combined where they entered from outside and pulled off their boots and coats before walking into the kitchen.

"Dinner should be ready in about thirty more minutes." Angela pulled plates and glasses down from the cabinets then rustled around in the silverware drawer.

"Angel. We really appreciate that you cooked for us. It smells like heaven, but don't think that we expect you to do that all the time. You have to be worn out from working all day." Randy smiled when she looked up at him.

"Really, it's not a problem at all. I don't like to cook for just myself. It's a waste of time. If I'm going to eat something good, I'll want to cook for more than just me. Really, I wouldn't go to the trouble for just me, so you're doing me a favor letting me cook for you sometimes."

"Hell, honey. If you want to cook for us, I'm sure not stopping you. I know a good thing when I smell it, and you're one hell of a cook." Randy winked at her.

Travis frowned at his brother. He didn't want her to think they were using her. Of course, Randy was right. She was one hell of a good cook. He sighed and shrugged. At least she hadn't run off after the mess they'd made earlier. Now all they had to do was slowly and carefully court her so that she didn't think they were just after her for sex. Since they'd screwed up already, it wasn't going to be easy to convince her that they were serious about her.

The fact that they did want her for more than just working in the office bothered him to some degree, but he brushed it aside. Their intentions were honorable. They weren't just looking for a quick roll in the hay or an easy screw when they felt like it. He was looking at forever and he was sure Randy was as well. Angela deserved only the best and he planned to give it to her.

Just seeing her bouncing around in their kitchen felt right to him. It made him think of home and family. He wanted to lean against her while she was washing dishes and rub over her blooming belly where their child would rest. Yeah, he had it bad for Angela.

Randy had that look on his face as well. His brother was a little in love with her already, judging by his expression as they watched her move around in the kitchen. Now came the hard part, convincing her that they were sincere in how they felt. It wouldn't be easy, but he hoped it would be fun.

When he tossed his and Randy's empty beer bottles in the trash, Angela announced that dinner was ready. He helped her carry it to the table and they all sat down to eat. As he cut into the meatloaf, he looked up at his brother across the table and found him smiling and staring at Angela. Their woman seemed relaxed now and was obviously happy sitting down with them to eat. Soon, he thought. Soon she would be comfortable with them hugging and kissing on her as she cooked or just because they wanted to. Soon.

* * * *

Angela willed her body to relax as they cleaned up the dishes together. The guys had refused to let her clean up by herself, and she had refused to leave it for them to do since she'd cooked. It didn't take long with the three of them working together. After drying her hands on a towel, Angela turned to tell the men good night.

"Night, guys. I'm heading to the cabin now."

"Wait. I'll walk you back." Travis disappeared into the laundry room but was right back carrying his boots.

"You don't have to walk me there. I know the way, and it's barely dark outside."

"Still, you don't need to be wandering around by yourself."

She gave up arguing with them and retrieved her jacket from the office. Randy walked them outside but sat in one of the rocking chairs on the porch as they walked down the steps. Angela wasn't sure what was going on with them. They had her completely confused.

Once she and Travis reached her little cabin, Angela said goodnight and smiled when he tipped his hat at her before she closed the door. She had to admit, both of the Woods men were handsome and well mannered. You didn't find that in a man very often anymore. Her ex had been nice enough, but he'd lacked even a smidgen of the polished appeal that Randy and Travis had. Neither had he been as intense as they had been when they had cornered her in the kitchen.

Angela poured a glass of iced tea and curled up in the plush club chair to think. They hadn't frightened her at all. She had no doubt that they would have stopped had she said the word, but all she could think about was that they were coming on to her because she had accepted a job with them and they were going to collect on that. Even though they definitely showed signs of being attracted to her, neither man had actually said anything that would suggest they expected her to *take care of them* sexually. Why had she said that?

Because I can't imagine one man, much less two wanting to have anything to do with someone like me for any other reason.

"Face it, Angela. You're poor white trash compared to them. What other possible motive would they have had?"

But wasn't she painting them as selfish, dishonest men if she thought they would use her that way? She didn't think they were sleazy like that at all. She had jumped to conclusions, not only embarrassing herself, but insulting them when they had been nothing but kind to her. She closed her eyes and sighed.

"I'm lucky they didn't fire me for that."

After sitting there for a while, she decided it was time for bed and headed to the bathroom to take a nice hot shower. It would help her relax so she would be able to sleep. As it was now, her body was still singing from the nearness of those two handsome men who'd revved her up earlier. Despite her efforts to put it all behind her, she could still feel the heat of their bodies as they'd leaned into her and smell their unique scents as if they were in the room with her.

She quickly stripped out of her jeans and shirt after stepping out of her tennis shoes. When she walked into the shower, the water pelted down on her with stinging warmth that helped to lessen the tension in her shoulders. As she soaped up her cloth and started to wash up, images of what the men might look like without their shirts on assaulted her. They would both be muscular without being bulky, their strength apparent in how they moved and the way their shirts moved over their bodies.

Angela drew in a deep breath as the need to trace each delineated line of their broad chests with her tongue made her weak in the knees. She could just imagine running her tongue around each flat nipple until they groaned in pleasure. Would they let her bite them? She shivered at the thought.

Without thinking about it, she slipped her hand between her legs and started sliding her index finger between her pussy lips over and over in a light caress. She was careful to avoid her clit since it was already so overly sensitive. She didn't want to come right away. Angela hadn't really felt like this in a long time, and she wanted to enjoy it, make it last.

She used her free hand to tease her nipples with the palm of her hand. Over and over she rubbed over first one and then the other until they were hard and poking out, eager for some attention. Wishing that Randy and Travis were there to suck on them, she lightly plucked at them one at a time while she began to tease her clit by running a finger around and around it. Soon she was desperate to come, her cunt tight with need and her pussy dripping with her juices.

Angela leaned back against the cool tiles and began pinching her nipples the way she knew would drive her crazy before finally letting her finger tap at her clit. She slowly added more pressure as she pushed against the hard nub between her legs until she was ready to cream. All it took was one pinch to her clit and she exploded with her orgasm, sliding down the tiled wall until she was resting on her heels in the bottom of the shower stall.

As soon as she had her breathing back under control, Angela stood up on shaky legs and rinsed off before shutting off the water and stepping out of the shower. The soft rasp of the oversized towel felt good against her skin except where it rubbed over her sensitive nipples. She quickly patted herself dry then pulled on the extra-large T-shirt she slept in. The soft material felt good to her skin as she climbed up into bed.

Though she had just climaxed only minutes earlier, Angela still felt needy. Her self-induced orgasms usually did the trick when she was aroused like she had been earlier, but this time, it only seemed to have reminded her that she didn't have what she really wanted between her legs—one or both of the Woods men. That could never happen. She wasn't their type, and they were way out of her league. Besides, they were her bosses, and she wasn't going to fuck her bosses.

"Get over it already. They're off limits. You've got to remember that, girl. All you'll end up doing is losing your job and more than likely your heart."

After what felt like hours of tossing and turning, Angela finally drifted off to sleep with thoughts of two delicious-looking cowboys dominating her dreams.

Chapter Seven

The next few weeks proved to be busy for Angela. She slowly got their office in order and caught up all of the bookkeeping issues they had either forgotten to do or put off on purpose. The inventory seemed to be in order, so all she had to do was keep it running smoothly and print out the weekly orders to be picked up by one of the ranch hands going into town.

She saw little of the guys during the week except at night when they came in to eat. She continued to cook their meals after she shut down the office each night. Angela worked Saturday mornings until noon, making sandwiches for the guys before she left for the day.

It was a relief that they were giving her some space to learn her way around the ranching business, but at the same time, she missed them. They had a way of filling the room with their presence. Without it, the house felt almost sad to her at times. Maybe she was projecting her own feelings though. She was coming to realize that she really liked them a lot more than she should.

The weekends, however, were another matter. After they finished for the day on Saturday, the men tended to stop by her little cabin for dinner and to talk. It had started off innocent enough when they stopped in when she'd just finished making spaghetti and a salad and she invited them to join her. After that, they continued to stop in for dinner and conversation before all three of them ended the evening on their porch enjoying the night sky.

Sundays they tended to take her around the ranch, showing her more about their home and what they did. Both men had hinted at how much easier it would be to ride out to look at some of the beautiful land they lived on, but so far they hadn't actually suggested taking a ride. Angela hoped they would bring it up again soon. She wanted to go horseback riding with them.

If she were being honest with herself, she would have to admit that she was growing more and more fond of Travis and Randy. Maybe even more than fond. She truly liked and respected them, and given how her body seemed to have a mind of its own whenever she was around them, Angela was pretty sure she was in lust with them as well. All it took was a glimpse of one of them for her pussy to moisten and her nipples to stand up and salute.

Shaking her head at the direction her thoughts had drifted, she decided that with it being Saturday and almost noon, she might as well go ahead and shut down for the day. Angela logged off the computer and straightened the desk before walking through the house to the kitchen. She'd just poured a glass of tea and was deciding what to fix the guys for lunch when the back door opened and closed. She stuck her head around the door to see Randy pulling off his boots.

"Hey. I was just about to start making sandwiches. I didn't expect you so soon." She watched as he shrugged off the jacket he was wearing.

"No need today. We're going into town for lunch. Got some errands to run."

Angela nodded and walked back into the kitchen to finish her tea before she headed back to her place. She couldn't help but wonder what errands they had that would take them into town. She wished she was going with them. It would be nice to get out of the cabin for a little while.

The back door opened and closed again as Randy walked into the kitchen. She guessed that Travis had made it. Randy walked over to the fridge and pulled out the tea then grabbed two glasses as well. Angela watched as he filled them with ice then tea. She took the pitcher from him and returned it to the refrigerator as he handed Travis his drink.

Angela smiled at them and rinsed out her glass before putting it in the dishwasher. It was time to go.

"See you guys later. Have a good time in town." She turned toward the living area and the front door.

"Hey, wait up. We want you to go with us, Angel. Thought you could use some time to shop, you know, get away for a little while." Travis drained the rest of his tea in one gulp.

Angela turned back around to face the men. "Um, thanks, but I'm sure you have plenty to do without carting me with you."

"Just a few errands. Since you've taken over the office, we have more time to do things we want to do now." Travis smiled at her. "Come on. You need to shop for some new clothes for one thing. You've only got a couple of outfits. I'm sure you get tired of washing them over and over again."

Angela cringed. They'd actually noticed that she wore the same three outfits every day. She had hoped they wouldn't notice. Guys normally didn't pick up on things like that. Besides, she didn't have a lot of money to buy much.

"Hey, honey. It's okay. We're not complaining or anything. We just thought you would like to shop. Most women like to shop." Randy walked over and pushed a loose strand of hair behind her ear.

"Um, I appreciate it, but I really don't have enough money yet to do much shopping. Maybe after I get paid again." She pasted a smile on her face and took a step back.

"What do you mean you don't have enough money to go shopping?" Travis asked with a scowl. "We've signed the payroll checks every week. You should have plenty to buy a few things."

"Um, I have plenty for now. I had to pay you back for the food and everything."

Randy and Travis's mouths flew open then closed almost at the same time. She could see how upset they were but didn't understand why. What had she done wrong?

"Come on." Travis took her elbow and guided her out of the kitchen and through the living area to the office.

Randy sat down in the office chair and booted up the computer. Angela had a bad feeling they weren't going to be happy with what she'd done. She had never expected them to find out this soon if at all. It wouldn't have mattered in another week or two. She would have had more money saved to buy what she needed by then.

"Good Lord, woman! You've taken way too much out of each check. No wonder you don't have any money. That stops right now! You don't owe us another cent. You've been cooking for us all this time. You shouldn't have taken a single dime out of your checks after the delicious meals you've served us." Randy started typing on the keyboard.

"What are you doing?" she asked.

"Cutting you another check to shop with. We owe you more than this for everything you've done for us. Don't even try to argue with us about it." He pointed a finger at her when he stood up to get the check from the printer.

Angela turned to Travis to make him understand that they didn't owe her anything for cooking when she'd been eating with them as well, but one look at his expression told her to quit while she was ahead.

"Here." Randy handed her the freshly signed check, daring her with his eyes to refuse it.

She sighed and took the check from him and folded it up and shoved it into her pocket. They were two of the most stubborn men she'd ever been around.

"Now let's go. We'll stop by your cabin so you can grab your purse or whatever you need." Travis kept one hand at the small of her back as they walked toward the front door.

"I can't believe you did that. You didn't leave yourself anything to live off of, Angel." Travis was still mumbling about it as he helped her climb up into the front seat of the big crew cab.

The drive into Riverbend was fairly quiet. Travis pointed out landmarks and people's homes as Randy drove. She slowly relaxed as the tenseness from earlier seeped away. She had all four checks in her pockets since she didn't own a purse. Randy said they would take her somewhere where they would cash her checks for her, but she needed to catch a ride into town the next time one of the hands were going to pick up supplies and open a checking account.

"You don't need to carry around a lot of cash or even keep it tucked away in the cabin," Travis said. "I trust everyone on the ranch without question, but you can't be too careful with strangers nowadays."

"What made you trust me?" she asked.

Travis looked at her with a smile. "I could just tell, Angel. Your eyes are as honest as anyone I've ever met."

She just shook her head. They were too trusting, she thought. Maybe she had been okay, but then he'd been a lifeline to her. Another person might have used them, but then maybe Travis wouldn't have been as generous with someone else. Maybe it was because he did trust her that he'd given her a chance.

When they finished cashing her checks at a gas station on the outside of Riverbend, Randy turned around and drove back into town, parking in front of the diner. It was close to two when they walked inside, so they had most of the place to themselves. Randy led them to a booth in the back. He and Travis waved at two men sitting at the counter.

Once they were seated, Travis pointed at the two men. "That's Sheriff Mac Tidwell on the left and Silas Atkins on the right. He's a deputy sheriff. They are both good men if you ever need anything."

"The sheriff and his brother, Mason, are married to Beth. Mason is an attorney here in Riverbend."

"B–both of them are married to her? I know you told me that you had two dads but isn't that illegal?" Angela had never heard of anything like that before she'd ended up in Riverbend.

"Technically, and on paper, she's married to the oldest but there is also another ceremony where they all pledge themselves to each other. There are a lot of ménage families here in Riverbend," Randy said.

"And they're all happy? No one gets jealous?"

"They're very happy. I'm sure there are problems like there are in any marriage, but they are equally important to Beth just like she's the most important person in their life." Travis seemed to be watching her very closely.

Angela wasn't one to judge. She would never say anything against something that she didn't understand. She had grown up in the heart of the Bible belt. She had obviously lived a fairly sheltered life. For an instant, she wondered about Travis and Randy. Did they plan to share a wife some day? Could she be a wife to two men at one time? She shoved that thought aside. It didn't really matter one way or another. She needed to concentrate on keeping a roof over her head and stop thinking about stuff like that. It would only get her into trouble.

"Hey, Randy, Travis. What can I get you guys today?" Mattie walked up with a broad smile on her face.

"Hey, Mattie. How are Nate and Bruce doing? Are they working today?"

"Nate's back there, but Bruce is running errands today. Hi, Angela. How are you doing?" Mattie smiled down at her.

"I'm doing fine, thank you."

She wasn't sure what to say to her now that she realized that the older woman was married to two men. She hadn't caught on to that the last time she'd been in the diner. Of course she had been all wrapped up in her own problems instead of paying attention to everything around her.

"So what will it be today?" She pulled out her pad to take their order.

They gave her their orders, and once she had returned with tea all around, Travis took up where they'd left off before Mattie had walked up.

"Angel, does it bother you that we have two dads?" he asked.

"No! I'm not judging anyone. I've just never heard of it before and wondered how that worked."

"Mom and the dads are happy and have been married for nearly thirty-seven years now. We have one older sister, Dee Ann, and one younger sister, Lauren," Randy added.

"You'll be meeting our parents before long. They usually come and visit about once every month or so. We go there for Thanksgiving and Christmas." Travis took a drink from his tea glass. "Mom's going to love you."

"Oh, well I doubt she will see that much of me. I'll be busy in the office. I won't get in the way," Angela assured them.

She didn't want the woman to get the idea she was after her sons. She wasn't a gold digger and didn't want anyone to think that of her. She needed to be sure and keep out of everyone's line of sight anytime they were visiting the men. Considering how attracted she already was to them, their mother would be sure to notice if she was always under foot.

"Nonsense, honey. You would never be in the way." Randy frowned at her.

"What are we doing next?" Angela quickly changed the subject.

"We need to see about some things at the feed and seed store. We thought you might enjoy browsing up and down the street while we're there. We could meet back at the truck at a specific time and then make a quick stop at the grocery store before heading back to the ranch." Travis glanced over at Randy as if to make sure that was fine with him.

"Okay. That sounds good. I doubt it will take me long to find a couple of tops and another pair of jeans."

She was still uneasy about the amount of money Randy had written that check for earlier. She was sure it was way more than what was correct. She was going to check it once she was back in the office on Monday. Until then, she didn't plan on spending much of it.

"You need a pair of heeled boots while you're shopping. If you're not sure what to get, wait for us and we'll help you pick them out," Randy said.

"Why do I need boots?" she asked.

"You're living on a ranch, honey. Not only do you need them for riding, but to protect your feet and lower legs from snakes and leftovers."

Angela looked over at Travis. "Leftovers? What are those?"

Travis grinned. "Leftovers are reminders of the last animal that might have passed by and left a little something for us to remember him by."

She frowned harder. "I don't get it."

Before Travis got a chance to explain, the answer hit her and she felt dense.

"Oh! You mean like scat or dung."

Travis chuckled. "That's right. It's a lot easier to hose off and clean up a pair of boots than it is sneakers, and you sure don't want to step in a pile in a pair of sandals."

Before she could argue about the need for a pair of boots, Mattie returned with their food. As they ate, Randy and Travis discussed the ranch while Angela listened, trying to learn from their conversation. When they'd finished, Randy settled the tab and they waved good-bye to Mattie before walking outside.

"We're going to park the truck by the feed and seed store since we have some parts to pick up. Just meet us back there in say"—Travis looked at his watch—"two hours. Will that give you enough time to do some shopping?"

"Oh, that's plenty of time. I'll probably be back before that."

"If you need us for anything, just call on your cell. You brought it with you, didn't you?"

"I've got it in my pocket." Angela patted her back pocket.

"Good. See you in a while, Angel." Travis squeezed her shoulder as they parted company.

Angela walked down the sidewalk, looking into the windows of the various stores as she passed. She saw several she would have loved to explore, but she didn't want to stop and take the chance that she got caught up in browsing and lost track of time. First she needed to buy what she had come for then she could stop in the other places if she had time.

The department store she stepped inside of near the end of the business district of Riverbend proved to be larger than she had expected. Instead of crowded aisles and disorganized shelves, the store was pleasantly arranged and comfortable to explore. She quickly located the women's section and found two pairs of jeans along with several nice blouses in her size. She stopped to look at a rack of slacks when someone walked up to her.

"Hi, I'm Bridgett. Can I take those for you so you can continue to look around?"

Angela turned, and a very pretty woman of about twenty-five with shoulder-length, wavy brown hair and pretty hazel eyes smiled back at her. Her smile was contagious. Angela felt her lips turn up as she nodded her head.

"Thanks. I'm not sure if I will buy anything else, but I do want to look around some more."

"You're new around here, aren't you?" Bridgett asked.

"Yeah. I'm working out on the Wood's Wilderness ranch outside of town."

"That's Travis's and Randy's place. You must be their office manager then. They've been looking for one for a long time. If I had been good with accounting, I'd have applied, but when it comes to keeping books, I'm hopeless."

Angela didn't know what to say to that, so she just smiled and nodded her head.

"Anyway, I'll have your things at the checkout whenever you're ready. If you need help finding something, just call for me." With that, the other woman turned and walked toward the back of the store.

After deliberating longer than she had planned on doing, Angela finally chose a pair of tan slacks that she thought would go with several of her new blouses. By the time she had checked out, she only had about forty minutes left before she was supposed to meet the guys back at the truck. She could probably stop and look around one of the stores on the way back.

She chose The Scent of a Woman to stop in and browse. Not only was the name intriguing, but the arrangement of body lotions and soaps in the window looked enticing. She had always loved it when she got scented soaps and lotions for Christmas or her birthday as a teenager. She hadn't owned anything like that in the last five or six years. She decided that splurging on a bottle of lotion wouldn't be too decadent.

As she sniffed some of the samples, a sales lady walked over and offered her a bottle to sample. Angela smiled and let her apply the lotion to the back of one hand. Once she had smoothed it in, she sniffed and instantly loved the fresh scent. It reminded her of vanilla and mint mixed together.

"That is wonderful!"

The other woman smiled. "It's new. We make all of the items right here in the store. This is called Warm and Tingly. The scented lotion comes in two sizes along with bath soap, bath salts, and a spritzer."

"Goodness. I hadn't planned to buy anything when I stopped to look around, but I don't think I can resist that lotion." Angela followed the striking woman to the other side of the store where an arrangement of the items was on display.

"Take your time and find what you like. I'm Grace. If you need anything, just holler."

Angela couldn't help but watch the woman walk back to the counter. She moved as gracefully as a ballerina. Her long jet-black hair hung almost to her waist. It flowed as she moved. With eyes the color of rich blue hues, her heart-shaped face and slightly upturned eyes gave her a very exotic appearance.

Shaking her head, Angela returned to gazing at the various offerings in the amazing scent before finally picking out a package that contained the body lotion and bath salts. She planned to return the next time she was in town and purchase the soap and spritzer as well. Checking the time on her phone, she realized she had spent far longer browsing than she had planned. She hurried over to the counter where she waited for Grace to ring up her purchases.

"Here you go. Inside the bag are a few samples for you to try. If you find you really like the scent you bought, there is a store across the street and down a block called Uniquely Yours that has candles in this same scent. It's sort of a new-age store run by Tish, Brian, and Andy. They are friends of mine. You should stop by their place as well."

"Thanks, but I'm supposed to be meeting my bosses to head back to the ranch. I'll plan to stop by the next time I'm in town though. Thanks." Angela took her bag and hurried out the door and down the sidewalk.

She passed another store she desperately wanted to explore called Jazzy Intimates. Going by the window display, it would seem that it specialized in lingerie. Angela had never actually owned anything remotely sensual or sexy in her life. She thought she would enjoy wearing something like that under her clothes. She would make sure to shop there the next time she came to town.

Angela arrived back at the truck just as Travis and Randy were adding bags to the backseat. She could see that they had sacks and boxes in the bed of the truck as well. When she walked up, Randy took her bags from her and carefully added them to the packages in the backseat.

"Did you get everything you needed?" he asked.

"I got everything I'd planned to get. There are some really nice stores here."

"We get tourists from all over the area visiting Riverbend to shop," Travis added.

"What about boots? I didn't see any boxes in your stuff." Randy's brows furrowed.

"Oh, I didn't have time to stop by a shoe store, so I thought I would look for a pair next time."

Travis and Randy exchanged glances but didn't say anything. She breathed a sigh of relief that they weren't making an issue of it. Instead, Travis helped her up to the front seat then Randy backed them out into the street. Instead of heading back toward the ranch, Randy drove a short ways down the road before parking in front of a couple of stores on the opposite side of the street.

"Come on. Let's take care of this real quick." Randy climbed out of the cab and waited as Travis helped her back down.

"Where are we going?" she asked.

"To find a pair of boots for you," Travis drawled.

Chapter Eight

Travis nearly ran into Angela when she stopped dead still in the middle of the sidewalk.

"What are you talking about? I told you I would get a pair when I come back to town." Her voice left no doubt that she was on the edge of being angry.

"No reason to wait 'til next time when we're here now. You need boots, Angela. You don't need to be walking around outside without them." Randy didn't even stop walking until he got to the store and opened the door only to find that they hadn't moved from beside the truck.

With an exasperated sigh, he let go of the door and stalked back to where Angela stood with her hands on her hips glaring at him. Travis couldn't help but grin. His brother didn't approve one bit that he wasn't saying anything. Travis wasn't a fool. He knew a fight was brewing and he would much rather stay out of it and be the one to soothe Angela's feathers afterward.

"Travis! Don't just stand there. Tell her to get her butt inside the store." Randy's voice had taken on a deeper tone.

"Randy. She isn't going to listen to me any better than she listens to you." He crossed his arms and waited for the fireworks.

Even he wasn't expecting what Randy did next. His brother scooped their office manager up and tossed her over his shoulder before stomping back to the store. Travis closed his mouth and followed behind them. He didn't want to miss this for anything. Since their Angel hadn't said anything yet, he could only assume she was as shocked as he was and would soon regain control of her mouth once again.

Sure enough, less than a minute later, Angela let Randy have it with both barrels. His brother had set her back down inside the store in front of the women's boots. She jammed her hands on her hips with flashing eyes and stomped her foot.

"You may be my boss at work, but you are *not* my boss outside of work. I am not buying boots today. And another thing, don't you dare manhandle me like that again!"

"First of all, Angela, I didn't manhandle you. I carried you into the store so you didn't have to walk. As for not being your boss outside of work, you are under mine and my brother's care since you live on our ranch and work for us. That means we are responsible for your well-being. We take that very seriously here in Riverbend. Women here are loved and cherished. We make sure that no woman in our area is abused or left without someone to take care of them. You need boots to protect you from twisting your ankle on rocks and in holes and from snakes. End of argument." Randy towered over their little angel with a matter-of-fact expression on his face.

Travis fought back a smile since he knew that neither his brother nor Angela would appreciate him finding humor in the situation. The fact that Randy was so interested in taking care of her told him that he definitely had feelings for the tiny woman. That went a long ways to settling the worry that he'd been harboring all these weeks.

Angela stared at Randy with an open mouth. She closed it then opened it before finally closing it and crossing her arms to stare at both of them.

"So, Angel. Are you ready to pick out a pair of boots?" Travis asked.

"I'm doing this under duress. I'm not sure I understand all of this mess about you being responsible for me. I can take care of myself. I've always taken care of myself."

"Well, now that you're here, you don't have to anymore, honey." Randy relaxed his stance and led her over to a chair. "Have a seat and we'll help you find something you like that fits well."

As if she had been waiting for them to settle things between them, Janie Ledbetter emerged from the back and smiled at them.

"Hi, boys. It's good to see you again. Who have you got here?" The robust older woman regarded their Angel with a knowing expression.

"This is Angela. She's our office manager out on the ranch. She needs a pair of boots," Randy told her. "Angela, this is Janie Ledbetter. She owns this store."

Angela smiled and started to get up to shake the woman's hand, but the store owner just shook her head and took her hand in a quick shake.

"Let's see what we can find for you. You look like you wear a size eight. Does that sound right?"

"Um, yes. That's right." Angela slipped off her shoes.

Over the next thirty minutes they hovered in the background while Janie helped Angela pick out a nice pair of boots that would serve to keep her safe. Travis knew that Randy had the ulterior motive of getting her on the back of a horse as soon as possible. They wanted their woman to be comfortable riding horses with them. It was another reason he knew Randy was falling for their angel.

Once they had paid for the boots, much to Angela's ire, they loaded back up in the truck to head back to the ranch. Travis was surprised when she didn't fuss all the way back about them buying the boots for her. He had the sneaking suspicion that she was mulling it all over in her head and would be addressing more than just the boots the next time she decided to confront them. He had no doubt that Randy would be ready for her.

He and his brother believed that a woman deserved to be pampered and taken care of. They didn't like seeing any female struggling or unhappy. It just went against their nature. Neither he nor his brother had ever allowed a woman to be abused or taken advantage of in their presence. It was only natural that now that they had found someone they were both attracted to that they would shower her with everything they could. The next step was to get Angela on board and get Randy to admit to his feelings for her.

When they pulled up outside of her cabin, Travis jumped down from the cab and helped Angela climb out. He helped her gather her purchases as well as the controversial boots before following her inside the cabin.

"Thanks for helping me and for letting me tag along on the trip." Angela set her packages on the coffee table.

"No problem. We wanted you to go with us, Angel. You weren't tagging along at all," Travis told her.

"Well, don't think that the conversation about the boots is over with by any means. I'm paying for the damn boots one way or another." She narrowed her eyes at him.

Travis wasn't getting in the middle of that with her. He would let Randy handle it. All Travis hoped was that his brother didn't make things worse when she made her case with him about the boots. Randy tended to be as stubborn as a mule and just as ornery. Sometimes he took it too far, and that was what had Travis worried.

"I'll let you and Randy hash that out. All we wanted to do was make sure you were safe, Angel. Your safety is very important to us." He pulled her into his arms and kissed her softly on the lips before she realized what he was doing. The soft brush of his lips across hers seemed almost surreal as he pulled back and strolled toward the door. "I'll see you later."

* * * *

Angela had him all tied up in knots. Randy picked up the box of supplies and carried it into the barn. He set it on the floor in the tack room and returned to the truck to get the next box, passing Travis on his way in with another box.

"She's stubborn and sassy," he said as they passed.

Travis didn't comment. Randy didn't expect him to. His brother knew how he was. He had to talk it out or he'd stay angry. He'd always been that way. Normally he was the quieter of the two unless he got truly angry about something. Then he had to talk it out to calm down. Otherwise it took a long, hard workout to settle him down.

As he carried another box into the barn, he passed the other man again coming out.

"She has no business walking around the ranch especially between the cabin and the house in nothing but sandals or a pair of tennis shoes. It's just too damn dangerous out here for that."

Still, Travis just nodded and kept walking. He knew his brother felt the same way he did about her safety. Why couldn't she accept that they wanted to make sure she was safe? What was so hard about letting them help her some? It wasn't like she was living off them. The woman worked hard. She took care of the office and she cooked for them most days. That was a lot of work as far as he was concerned.

"Besides, if we're going to get her on the back of a horse anytime soon, she needs good boots to wear." Randy was waiting on Travis when he returned from the barn having made the last trip of supplies. "Do you agree with me?"

"Of course I do. I just think you might want to back off a bit from your demanding personality. She's not used to it and obviously wasn't raised where women were cherished like we do here in Riverbend."

Randy grimaced. He hadn't thought about it like that. All he could think about was how much he wanted to keep her safe and happy. Of course being mad wasn't being happy, and she was mad at him right then. He sighed and nodded.

"You're right. I can be a little bossy when I'm worried about something."

"Brother, that is the understatement of the year," Travis said with a chuckle. "You are the most controlling person I've ever met. Just tone it down some."

Well, his brother would know. He'd been telling him what to do most of his life. He was just lucky that Travis didn't take exception to it. His brother had an alpha personality as well, but didn't seem to mind letting his younger brother do the bossing. Maybe Randy needed to think about that some. Was he being disrespectful of his older brother with how he always took the lead and tried to order the other man around? Why did he feel the need to call all the shots? Why did Travis let him?

He looked over at the other man as he drove the truck back up to the house. He didn't seem the least bit uncomfortable or upset about anything. It was something he needed to think about.

"What do you think about having some friends over next weekend? We're pretty much out of calving season now. It would be nice to cook out and just hang out with everyone for a while." Travis opened his door and stepped down from the truck.

Randy climbed down from the cab and walked around to the other side and climbed the steps to the porch behind his brother. Travis walked over and sat in one of the rockers. He sat in one of the others. Maybe that wasn't such a bad idea.

"Sounds like a plan to me. Who all do you want to invite?"

Travis stared off in the direction of where Angela's cabin was nestled among the trees and bushes.

"Jared, Quade, and their wife Lexie, maybe Mac, Mason, and Beth. Who else do we know?" He turned and looked at Randy.

"There's Brody and Lamar and their new wife, Caitlyn. Her brother and his partner and wife. I think their names are Andy, Brian, and Tish."

"What?" Travis asked when Randy narrowed his eyes at his brother.

"They are all in ménage relationships. You didn't list any traditional couples."

"Well, neither did you. I just think it would be a good idea to introduce Angela to them and get her used to the way things are around here. That's all."

Randy cocked his head at his brother. "We agreed to take it slow with her, Travis. She's not used to our way of life, and she's also getting over a failed relationship where she was being used. I don't know if shoving the lifestyle down her throat like this is a good idea just yet."

"I think she's stronger than you give her credit for being, little brother. Angela knows what's going on around Riverbend. She isn't naive."

"Still, seeing it around town when she's there and being bombarded with it from all sides at a cookout might be a little much." Randy sighed, looking out over the ranch he and Travis had worked so hard on these last few years. "I don't know. Maybe you're right. Maybe I'm not giving her enough credit. I'll leave the invitations up to you. You're better at that stuff than I am."

"Only because I've had plenty of practice while you spend all your time out on the ranch. Don't worry, little brother. I know all about how you like to hide from people. That's going to all change when we claim Angela. You know that, don't you?"

Randy ignored his brother's smirk. "I don't hide from anyone. It takes work to keep a ranch going. Someone has to ride the fences and check the herd."

"Which is why we have ranch hands. You do entirely too much for the number of men we employee. Time to back off some, Randy. We're going to have a wife to take care of soon. You might as well start releasing the reins some and letting our foreman do more of his job."

Randy frowned over at his brother before returning his gaze to the corrals where one of the hands was exercising one of the horses. He made a mental note to tell the young man that he needed to watch how close he rode to the fence. Butterscotch was famous for crowding the fence. He could get his foot trapped and get pulled off the horse.

"Are you paying any attention to me at all, Randy?" Travis asked, cutting into his thoughts.

"Of course I am." He knew it came out a little harsher than he'd intended, but Travis was used to his gruff disposition. Still…

"I'm leaving the food aspect of this to you and Angela. You two can decide what to cook and work together on putting it together. I'll take care of the guest list and making sure they all get invited."

"Sounds like you're getting the easy part of this to me." Randy smiled at his brother.

"You bet, little brother. All I have to do is make some phone calls. Too bad you're not so good with making nice with people. If you were, you could have been the one chatting up our friends."

"Yeah, but I get the best part of it anyway. I get to spend time with Angela and you don't." Randy couldn't believe that he had the childish urge to stick his tongue out at his brother.

He couldn't stop the grin from spreading across his face at the thought. Being able to tease with Travis felt good. It dawned on him that they hadn't really just relaxed and enjoyed each other's company in a long time—too long.

"You just had to bring that up, didn't you?" Travis asked.

"Well you're the one who decided to take the easy way out. I deserve some form of compensation for having to deal with the food."

"Yeah, right. Tell me you're not going to pawn it all off on Angela to handle and all you do is carry the bags and fire up the grill."

"She likes to cook. I'm not going to get in her way with something she enjoys. I'll handle the grilling and she can do whatever she wants with the rest."

Randy grinned at how hard Travis had to work to keep a straight face. The scowl he was mangling looked more like he smelled something nasty and was trying to hide it. The look was not becoming on his big brother.

"Just remember that she's mad at you right now about those boots. You'd do well to be nice to her when you ask her to help you with the cookout." With that Travis stood up and stretched. "I'm going to go fix something for us to eat. You be thinking about how you're going to grovel and beg for her to help you."

"Yeah, fuck you, too, brother." Randy grimaced.

He hadn't thought about having to ask her for her help. Travis was right. She wasn't going to be too accommodating considering how mad she was right then. Maybe she would have had time to cool off if he waited to ask her Sunday night or Monday morning. He pondered the problem while he waited for Travis to yell that dinner was ready.

If he waited until Monday, something could come up on Monday to keep him busy all day so that he wouldn't be able to talk to her until that night. He didn't think he wanted to wait that long. They would need to decide on what food to cook and then make out a grocery list and go to town to fill it. No. It would be much better to get it over with on Sunday. He'd go over and talk to her Sunday afternoon.

With that decision out of the way, he let his mind wander while he waited for dinner. As much as he liked Angela and was probably even a little in love with her, Randy wasn't sure she would accept both him and his brother as her men. Not everyone was cut out for the ménage lifestyle. Getting hurt again wasn't something he wanted to repeat. Maybe this cookout would be a good way to determine how open Angela would be to that type of arrangement.

He couldn't stop the thought of her between him and Travis from torturing him as he sat there in the dwindling evening light. She would feel good there where they could both touch her and kiss her. The feel of her ass nudged against his cock had him reaching to adjust his suddenly tight jeans. What he wouldn't give for five minutes of just holding her in his arms, kissing her sweet lips. The way her breasts jutted out when she was angry made him groan. He wanted to taste those ripe berries that were sure to grace such magnificent breasts.

He would mold and squeeze the delightfully full globes as he licked and teased the taut nipple before drawing it into his mouth and sucking on it with everything he had. He could just imagine her sweet cries as she drew nearer to her orgasm. His brother would be giving her other breast the same attention. He could almost feel her soft skin beneath his hand, taste how sweet her plump nipple would be.

"Randy! Dinner is ready."

Travis's voice jerked him out of his head. He had his hand at his crotch, rubbing his stiff dick through his jeans with the heel of his hand. He figured he should feel guilty fantasizing about Angela and messing with himself, but he didn't. She was one of the sexiest women he'd ever seen. Soon they would have the real thing in their arms and hopefully in their bed.

Chapter Nine

Angela pushed her hair from her eyes as she bent over the little oven and pulled out the chicken pot pie she'd made. Weekends were the only time she actually cooked in the little cabin. As small as the kitchen was, it still worked fine for her. She placed the casserole dish on the top of the stove and closed the oven door. She had made enough that she could take it to work with her and they could have the leftovers for lunch the next day providing the guys didn't eat it all at dinner that night.

Placing the hand mitts back on the counter, she opened the fridge and pulled out a pitcher of tea and reached for a glass. A knock on the door startled her. She quickly set the pitcher and glass on the counter and walked across the room to open the door. Randy stood outside with a smile on his face.

"Hey. Is something wrong?" she asked.

He frowned. "No, why would you think something's wrong?"

"I guess the fact that Travis isn't with you makes me thing something is wrong."

"Um, can I come in?"

"Oh, sorry. Sure. Come on in. Would you like some tea? I was just about to pour myself a glass." Angela stepped back to let the big man past.

"No thanks, but you go ahead. I can smell whatever you cooked for dinner from here. Smells real good." Randy walked with her over to the little bar.

"I just took it out of the oven. It's got to sit and cool off before we eat." She poured the tea then returned it to the fridge.

Angela wondered why Randy was there without Travis. As angry as she had been about the boots the day before, she didn't feel that way anymore. All it had taken was to step outside that morning to carry the trash to the big can they kept secured from animals and finding a snake along the way for her to be thankful she was wearing her new boots. She had all but stepped on the damn thing before she heard the rattles.

They sat there in silence for a few long seconds before Randy finally cleared his throat and spoke up. Angela held her breath, wondering why Travis hadn't come, leaving Randy to tell her something important. Were they going to fire her?

"Travis and I are planning to have some friends over next weekend, and we were hoping you'd help with setting up the food."

Angela let out her breath in a soft *whoosh*. Why was Randy asking her something so simple without Travis? Surely he wasn't angry with her over the boots. If anyone was going to still be angry, she would have thought it would be Randy.

Relaxing, she smiled. "Sure. I'd love to help you. What did you have in mind? I can cook most anything. How many will there be besides you guys?"

"I'm going to cook hamburgers on the grill, so nothing fancy. There will be about twelve other people besides the three of us."

Angela frowned. The three of them? What did he mean by that? Were they going to have a girlfriend with them? She decided to let it go. It wasn't any business of hers. The fact that she'd allowed herself to become so attached to them, letting her hormones come out and play, didn't mean that she meant anything to them. She was only their office manager and evidently, their cook. Besides, it was a way for her to pay them back for the boots without starting another argument.

"Okay. So we need to make out a grocery list. Hold on and let me get some paper. I'll be right back." She hurried into her bedroom and searched for her tablet that she often made notes on. When she returned, Randy was still sitting at the little island.

"Usually you get about two nice-size patties out of a pound of hamburger meat. So that means we'll need between ten and twelve pounds of meat to make sure all of the men get two burgers."

She and Randy made out the list, deciding on potato salad, baked beans, and coleslaw. By the time they got through, she was sure the chicken pot pie would be cool enough to eat.

"Are you sure you don't want some dinner? It's chicken pot pie. I was expecting both you and Travis for dinner tonight." Inwardly she cringed at how that sounded.

It was almost a reprimand that they weren't eating with her. She'd allowed herself to count on their visits and meals together. She would have to stop allowing her rampant hormones to rule her head before she got herself into trouble.

"I'll pass as good as it smells. Travis was cooking our dinner tonight. If I don't do it justice, he might refuse to cook anymore, and then I'd starve."

"I hardly think you would starve, Randy. Surely you can open a can of soup and warm it up," she teased.

"A can of soup wouldn't touch my hunger. I'm more of a meat-and-potatoes man. Soup would just whet my appetite." He grinned at her. "I better be going."

As if he realized that she didn't understand why they were suddenly eating at home instead of with her, he turned back around and looked down at her with a sincere expression.

"We figured we'd been intruding on your alone time too much lately and wanted to give you some space. Otherwise we'd be scarfing up that chicken pot pie tonight, Angela. I don't want you to think we were tired of your cooking or your company or anything." He smiled and winked.

Angela couldn't help but smile back as she walked him to the door. "Here's your list. Let me know if there's anything else you need for me to take care of."

"I will. I figure we can go pick up the groceries on Friday afternoon if that's okay with you."

"Oh. Sure, I'll be happy to go along with you."

"Of course you're going with me. I'd never know how to pick out the right food, especially if it involves picking out anything fresh. I'm terrible at that part of shopping. I can throw some TV dinners in the cart as easily as anyone, but I never learned the fine art of squeezing something without squishing it all over me."

Angela couldn't help but chuckle over the thought of Randy with the remains of an orange or a cantaloupe all over him.

"Somehow I picture you as the kid who shakes all the bags and boxes under the Christmas tree. Am I right?" she asked.

He laughed. "You've found me out. I'm a closet package shaker all right. So is Travis though."

They had reached the door across the room and Randy rested his hand on the doorknob. Instead of immediately opening the door, he turned back to her, searching her face as if he was looking for something. She felt as if he was staring into her soul when he looked into her eyes. Before she knew what he was going to do, Randy bent over her and wrapped one hand around the back of her neck before covering her lips with his.

She gasped, and he took that opportunity to slip inside her mouth with his tongue, stroking her from the inside out. He licked along the roof of her mouth then pulled back to leave soft kisses all along her cheek and jaw before returning to her lips. The pressure of his lips against hers had her heart skipping even as the depth of his kiss left her pussy clenching and wet with her juices.

When he slowly pulled back, Angela was sure she looked as shocked as she felt. He smiled a slow smile that always turned her heart inside out. It transposed his entire face into something that was beyond handsome. She swallowed and started to speak, though what she was planning on saying she didn't have a clue, but Randy stopped her with a finger to her lips.

"I'll talk to you tomorrow, honey. Go eat your dinner before it gets ice cold." He turned and walked out the door before closing it behind him.

Angela locked it then slowly walked back to the kitchen area. What was going on? She'd told them she wouldn't sleep with them. Sure, she was attracted to both of them, but that was ludicrous and besides, they were her bosses. She wasn't sleeping with her bosses. She could admire them and, okay, maybe even have sexual fantasies about them alone in her bed at night, but anything more was out of the question. Besides, hadn't he alluded to having a girlfriend with them at the cookout next weekend? Why had he kissed her like that when he was going to be seeing another woman?

Without really thinking about it, she fixed herself a plate and poured more tea before settling down at the small bar to eat. All she could think about was the kiss. It had been magical to say the least. Still, she had to stay strong. They were off limits, though right then, she wasn't sure why anymore.

After cleaning up in the kitchen, Angela ran her bath water and sprinkled some of her new bath salts in the tub. Stepping into the almost hot bathwater felt like heaven. She eased down into the tub and leaned back to soak. Immediately the kiss came back to haunt her, and she found her hands moving of their own accord. She lightly rubbed over her breasts before scraping her nails against her nipples until they were hard and aching. The throb of her pulse beat in her cunt, making her squirm in the warm water.

Angela moved a hand down to her needy pussy and let her fingers slide between her southern lips over and over until she was craving more. She continued to pluck and pull on her nipples with one hand as she circled her clit with a finger from her other one. She couldn't stop her pelvis rocking in the water as she felt the heat from her arousal building all over her body.

She thought about the two men in the house up the rise and wished they were there with her. One would play with her breasts, mounding them and licking or nipping at her nipples, while the other would go down on her, teasing her clit with his tongue. She would run her hands through their hair as they pleasured her together. God, how she wanted to feel Randy's hands on her breasts. He'd know how to squeeze her and pull on her nipples. Maybe he would even bite the hard little nubs as his brother sucked on her clit and made her come.

She thrust two fingers deep inside her cunt as she rubbed her clit with her thumb. The dual sensations along with her pulling and pinching on her nipples shot her over the edge like a rocket, but once the sensations settled down, the emptiness returned. Angela sighed and sat up to finish bathing. Playing with herself always left her with a vague sense of emptiness instead of the relief it was supposed to bring her.

* * * *

"Well? What did she say?" Travis asked when Randy walked into the kitchen.

"She said she'd be glad to help us with the food. We made a grocery list." He pulled the list out of his pocket. "I'm going to take her into town Friday afternoon to buy groceries."

"Perfect! This is going to be great. She'll see that there are a lot of people around here in ménage relationships and when we start talking to her about it maybe she won't be as reluctant about it."

"I still don't think it's going to work out like that. I think she's more hung up on our being her bosses than she is about there being two of us."

"The more we treat her like a woman and less like our office manager, the more she'll get used to it, and when we tell her how we feel, it won't come as such a shock." Travis carried the spaghetti he'd made over to the table where the plates and silverware were already waiting.

Randy sat down across from him. He could tell his brother didn't share his optimism about the situation. Maybe he wasn't as positive as he let on, but one of them had to appear confident. Besides, Travis already knew he was in love with their angel. She was perfect for them. They just had to convince her of that. He needed his brother on his side. Randy might be the more aggressive one, but when it came to matters of the heart, it was up to Travis to keep things going smoothly. His arrogant brother was like a bull in a china shop when it came to relationships.

"Did she give you a hard time about the boots?" Travis asked.

"Nope. She didn't bring it up at all. In fact, she was wearing them. I wanted to remind her not to wear them too much at first or she'd end up with blisters, but I figured I might better keep my mouth shut on that one."

"You're learning, little brother."

"Have you gotten in touch with everyone about the cookout?"

"Yep. Looks like everyone will be there unless something happens. I think they're all excited about it, too." Travis figured that Caitlyn would be more than happy to get out for a while.

Her husbands, Brody and Lamar had gotten so overprotective it was almost comical. Ever since she'd found out she was pregnant, they had put her on lockdown and wouldn't let her do anything without one of them with her. He almost felt sorry for her. Caitlyn handled their taxes for them. He was sure she would be extremely grateful that they had managed to finally land an office manager. Their paperwork had been a complete mess for her to have to deal with for last year's return.

"What are you grinning about over there?" Randy asked.

"Just thinking about how crazy Brody and Lamar are right now trying to smother Caitlyn in cushions and cotton to keep her safe."

His brother chuckled and nodded his head. "You're right about that. I've never seen those two act like this before. It's funny as hell."

"By the time the baby comes, she's going to be a head case. I'm surprised she hasn't taken a piece of some of that iron they deal with in their shop to their heads by now." Travis wondered how he and Randy would feel when Angela carried their baby.

Suddenly the room felt hot and his hands shook. *Fuck!* What was he doing? A picture of her round with their babe flashed in his head, and he felt sick with worry. How would they ever be able to keep her safe? Then he thought about the miracle of life she would hold inside of her near her heart. One they had helped to create. Waiting for her to get used to them was going to suck big time. He didn't want to wait. He wanted to fill her with their seed right now.

"What's wrong?" Randy started to stand up with his empty plate in his hand.

"Nothing. I just thought about what I'd feel like when we manage to get Angela pregnant. It's a little scary and cool at the same time."

"Don't put that thought in my head. I don't need it right now. I'm barely able to keep my hands off of her as it is."

"Well don't screw this up by jumping the gun, little brother. She's our future." Travis followed Randy into the kitchen with his plate and glass.

"Um, I kissed her before I left."

Travis sighed. He should have known Randy wouldn't be able to resist temptation for long. Once Randy got something in his head, he had no patience. This was going to be hard to make work with him stealing kisses all the time.

"You know you're going to screw things up if you push her too fast. You said it yourself, she's not ready to brush aside that we're her bosses yet."

"Hell, I couldn't resist her. She was looking up at me with those pretty blue eyes and kissable lips. I had to have a taste."

"What did she taste like?" Travis wished he'd been there to steal his own kiss.

"Like heaven. Her lips are soft and perfect. I want more, Travis. It's going to be hard as hell to resist her this week."

"Well suck it up. She's off limits while she's at work right now. Later, when we've gotten her more used to us, we'll push her some."

They washed the dishes up in silence. Travis figured his brother was reliving that kiss he'd managed to get. He was hard as a rock from thinking about her with their baby planted in her belly. Nothing would please him more than to hold her and feel the baby kick. Of course, burying himself inside of her would rank a close second right about now.

As soon as they finished cleaning the kitchen up, he and Randy headed to bed. Mornings came early on a ranch, and Monday mornings proved to be the toughest.

When he stepped into the shower several minutes later, Travis thought about Angela and how pretty her golden-red hair was when she left it loose instead of pulling it back into a ponytail. He was sure it got in her way when she was working, but he ached to see it spread out on his pillow while he was pleasuring her. That thought alone drew a moan from him. He immediately grasped his rock-hard cock in his hand and stroked it from base to tip.

He'd been semi-hard for her ever since he'd found her on the side of the road. Now, after thinking about her kissing his brother and filled with their baby, he was so hard he ached from it. His balls felt tight as he gripped his dick, pumping up and down in a long slow glide. He couldn't help but picture Angela on her knees at his feet with her hands splayed out on his thighs as he slowly fed his cock into her hot, wet mouth one inch at a time. Her plump lips would stretch wide around his girth as he sank deep into her mouth.

He squeezed the base of his shaft before pulling on it over and over as he imagined her digging her nails into his thighs while he fucked her pretty mouth. His grip grew tighter as he jerked on his cock. His balls grew tighter to the point of pain. Travis groaned as fire raced down his spine to gather at the base in preparation of his orgasm.

Angela's eyes would stare up into his as he filled her mouth with his straining cock. She would swallow around his dick as he hit the back of her throat, massaging the spongy helmet as she gently massaged his balls with one hand. All it would take was one moan from her against his shaft and he would lose it.

Travis pumped his dick harder, straining against the need to come, wanting to prolong it as he savored the idea of Angela touching him, loving him as much as he loved her. Just the thought of her groaning around his hard, thick shaft did it for him. His balls ignited as he spewed ribbons of cum over his hand and against the tiles at the back of the shower stall. The muscles of his ass tightened to the point of pain as he stood on tiptoe with the power of his orgasm. Nothing had ever felt that intense before. He couldn't imagine what it would be like once he and his brother finally had her between them.

He leaned on one hand propped on the tiles while he fought to slow his breathing and still his racing heart. As soon as he could stand up without shaking, Travis cleaned up and stepped out of the shower to dry off. He had no doubt he would sleep tonight, but he would dream of golden-red hair and startling blue eyes.

Chapter Ten

The week flew by as Angela fielded phone calls and handled the accounts. She was learning more and more every day about ranch life and the intricacies of breeding cattle. The idea of having to make sure you didn't inbreed too much or the meat wouldn't be good to eat or that the resulting cows would be more susceptible to disease had never crossed her mind before. It was a very complicated process to keep up with breeding records. Then there was the piece that meant keeping up with the different feeds and stock prices for them. She sometimes felt as if her head would explode.

Each night when they sat down to eat dinner, they filled her in on what was going on around the ranch. She found out they were working on a small horse breeding business to supply cutting horses to the area. Evidently good cutting horses were often hard to find. Travis confessed that it was something else he needed to show her so he could turn over the paperwork to her to keep up with. They hadn't been kidding about it being a fast-paced position.

One or both of the men would walk her to her cabin each night to make sure she arrived safely at her door. They touched her often outside of work and always left her with a kiss. She realized that she was getting comfortable being around them and their touch, which worried her. She already cared about them more than was healthy. Deep down, she knew it might even be love, but she refused to let herself think about it. They were her bosses, and she couldn't risk screwing up the wonderful life she had. There was no doubt in her mind that if she gave in to her feelings and let them talk her into having sex with them that eventually she would lose her job when they moved on. And they would move on. Angela wasn't the sort of woman men like Randy and Travis would eventually settle down with.

She didn't even bother to think about the fact that there were two of them. She would only need to think about that aspect if she were going to get serious about them, which she refused to do.

Friday at lunch time, the brothers walked into the kitchen, arguing over a horse for some reason. They rarely argued over anything as far as Angela knew, but evidently this horse was a major issue for them.

"I'm telling you, Travis, that mare isn't a good investment. She's headstrong. Breeding her will be difficult, and we don't know how she'll react to the foal once it's born."

Travis shook his head. "You're not looking at the whole picture. Sure, she's a little feisty, but she's strong and has excellent blood lines. She's also got good instincts that will pass on to the foal."

"If she'll even carry it. You know as well as I do that if a mare is too rowdy they tend to miscarry."

Travis sighed and dried his hands on a towel as Randy washed his. Angela kept quiet. She found that she learned a lot about not only the ranch but about the men themselves if she just listened and didn't interrupt when they did have an argument.

Where Travis was more animated about things in general, he also tended to be the more levelheaded of the two. Randy seemed calmer on the surface because it took more to get him riled, but still waters run deep, and never had that been more true than with the younger of the two men. He took things very seriously and would often storm out of an argument to go let off some steam.

Now they walked over to the table, shelving their argument until later, evidently. They sat down to eat and changed the subject. Angela just shrugged it off and asked after the various hands she had met over the last weeks. She knew that Buzz and his wife were expecting their first child and Homer, their foreman, and his wife, Hazel, were proud grandparents. The men filled her in on the gossip around the ranch as they ate.

"Homer said they've come across some cat tracks out on the western part of the ranch near the canyons. He hasn't seen anything to indicate it is hunting our area, but we need to keep watch." Travis picked up his glass and took a drink of tea.

"Wow! I hadn't thought about there being wild animals around. Do you see many when you're out riding?" Angela asked.

"Actually, we don't see as many as you would think. There are a few wolves in the area, but they mostly stay away from the cows. As long as hunting is good in the area for them, they don't bother us. I haven't seen a cougar on our ranch at all, but we saw them a few times at home when we were growing up," Randy said.

"I thought they were called mountain lions." Angela frowned.

"That's another name for them. They're also called pumas. We just call them cats." Travis grinned at her. "Not to be mixed up with the barn cats and their kittens."

Angela instantly sat up straighter. "You have kittens here?"

Randy shook his head. "Now you've done it. She's going to want to go see them."

"Of course I want to see them! I love animals and always wanted a cat. I've just never lived anywhere I could have one."

Travis's smug smile directed at his brother told her he had brought it up on purpose. Angela didn't care if he was poking at his brother using her this time because it involved kittens. She briefly wondered if she could talk them into letting her have one of them in her cabin.

"Take her out to see them before you go to town for groceries, Randy. She'll get a kick out of them." Travis began cleaning off the table.

"Oh, hell no! You're going with us to see them. I'm not doing this alone." Randy stood up and helped Travis.

Angela stood up, knowing her smile probably covered her face. She hadn't been this excited since she'd gotten the job working for them. Even if they wouldn't let her keep one in the cabin, she was sure they would let her go play with them as long as she didn't get in the way of the ranch hands doing their jobs.

"While we're out there, let's show her the horses, too," Randy suggested.

"Good idea. Angela, we want to teach you how to ride. We have a couple of horses picked out for you to choose from. They're both gentle mares and will be perfect mounts for you to learn on." Travis loaded the dishwasher as she wiped off the table.

"I'd love to go riding. I've actually ridden a few times when I was a teenager, but I'm not a true horsewoman."

The men exchanged looks that Angela couldn't decipher. What were they thinking? She often wondered if they could talk to each other mentally the way they exchanged looks at times. Usually it was when they didn't want to say something around her. It often made her angry. She didn't like for people to talk about her behind her back.

There had been a lot of that when she'd lived in Belzoni, especially after her parents had died and she'd struggled to work and go to school. There had been a lot of talk that she was sleeping with someone for money and that had been both demeaning and cruel to treat her that way when she wasn't hurting anyone. She'd often thought it was because she was trying to make something of herself by finishing junior college and getting a degree. Most of the girls there didn't have the money or the drive to go any farther than high school. They got married and had kids. There was nothing wrong with that if it was what you wanted. Angela wanted more than that though. She wanted to be able to take care of herself if she found herself on her own again, which was how she ended up working for Travis and Randy.

"Are you ready to go meet the horses?" Randy asked.

"And the kittens," she added with a mischievous grin.

* * * *

Travis couldn't wait to get their Angel up on a horse. She would look great riding around the ranch between them. The more they integrated her into their everyday lives, the easier it would be to court her in earnest later. He knew Randy was getting impatient. They both wanted her in their bed sooner rather than later, but anything worth having was worth waiting for. Angela was definitely worth waiting for.

They walked out the back door from the laundry-mudroom toward the second set of stables. It housed the horses they wanted to show Angela. The other one held mostly working horses. They would check out the kittens last. He had no doubt she would want to take one home with her. Neither of them had any problem with that. It would give her a greater sense of home. He was all for anything that got her to thinking of the ranch as home.

"Here we are." Randy walked up to a pretty bay mare with her head leaning over the stall door. "This is Sunshine. She's ten years old and is as sweet as cotton candy."

Angela walked up to the mare and held out her hand for the horse to sniff her. Then she slid her hand over the horse's forehead and along her neck.

"She's beautiful. What a pretty color." She rubbed both hands over the horse's body and talked to her in a soft, lilting voice that had Travis wishing he was the mare with all of her attention focused on him.

"Come down here, Angela. This is Gracie. She's a little less docile, but not too spirited for you to handle." Randy held her bridle as Angela walked up to the slightly larger mare.

"What color is she? It's amazing!" She held out her hand as she had for the other horse then ran her hand along the smooth neck.

"She's a blue roan. That's a black horse with white hairs interspaced throughout her coat. I normally only see this on males, but she is the perfect example of a true blue roan."

"I've never seen anything like her. She's amazing." The horse nudged her shoulder.

Angela laughed and cooed to her as she rubbed all over the mare. This one definitely had more spirit and seemed to like her. Travis could see which one she had picked. When she turned to tell them, he nearly came just from the look of pure happiness on her face.

"I guess you know who I want to ride, don't you."

"Yep. I'd say that was pretty obvious." He chuckled. "Randy was sure you'd pick her."

"Why the name Gracie?" Angela asked.

"When we first got her, we placed her in a stall next to one of our geldings we'd named George Burns because he was such a comedian. He was always into something and could open any gate or stall we had. Well, she immediately took a liking to him and constantly *talked* to him. He'd look over at her and shake his head like he was trying to figure out what she was talking about. The name just stuck, Gracie and George Burns." Randy chuckled.

"Where is George now?" she asked.

Travis grinned. "George was nearly fourteen then. We gave him to Homer for when his grandkids are visiting. They love him and he seems to love them as well. He sure keeps everyone on their toes and in stitches with his antics."

"That's sweet. Did Gracie miss him?"

"I don't think so. She still tends to talk a lot when you take her out to ride. You'll see." Travis took her hand to draw her away from the mare's stall. "Let's go see the kittens, and then you two need to head to town so you can get back before it gets too dark to unload the groceries."

As he pulled her toward him, Gracie let out a snort and settled her head over Angela's shoulder as if trying to keep her there. Angela giggled and turned to hug the mare, telling her she would be back to visit soon.

Randy led them over to the storage barn where they kept the grain and hay. A couple of tomcats scrambled out of their way as they walked inside the barn. The sweet smell of hay was far more appealing than the more earthy smell of horse and manure from the stables. He followed as his brother took Angela's hand and led her over to where several bales of hay made a natural enclosed area off to one side. There were two mother cats tending to their kittens inside the enclosure. He waited to see how Angela would react when she first saw them.

She slowly leaned over with Randy and immediately gasped with delight. Travis couldn't take his eyes off of her as she lay over the hay bales and looked at the squirming mess of kittens he'd found a few days before. The sight of her rounded ass up in the air was almost more than he could stand. He adjusted his cock in his jeans and walked closer to them.

"What do you think? Look like little rats, don't they." Travis loved teasing her.

"No they don't! They're adorable. I can't believe the two momma cats are raising them together like this. They look to be almost the same age."

Randy spoke up. "I think the calico over there had hers about four days before the orange one did."

"What are the momma cat's names?" she asked as she watched the kittens play together.

"Uh, momma cats," Randy said.

She huffed out an annoyed breath and bumped his shoulder. "That's terrible. They should have their own names. How old are the kittens?"

"The first batch will be six weeks old tomorrow and the others are about four days behind." Randy reached down and picked up a calico ball of fur and sat it on the hay bale between them.

"She's so cute. Oh look! She's hissing at you, Randy." The furry creature was jumping up and down sideways hissing at the man.

Travis chuckled. "He should be cozying up to him instead. Randy is the reason they all have extra food and fresh milk each morning."

"Aw, that's so sweet, Randy." She put the little kitten back with the others and randomly rubbed over all of them.

One fuzzy orange runt climbed over the others to reach her hand. It latched on to her thumb and tried to chew on it. She giggled and pulled him out to cuddle him. Holding him up so she was eye to eye with the creature, Travis watched as she rubbed it against the side of her face and talked to it. Yep. She'd ask for this one, he was sure of it. He and Randy exchanged glances. His brother's eyes seemed almost misty.

"Um, Travis. Do you think I could have one of them? I'd take good care of him and clean up after him." She didn't look at either of them as she caressed the kitten.

"You'll have to talk to Randy about that. They're his domain, not mine."

She turned to Randy, gave him the biggest wide-eyed look he'd ever seen, and poked out her lips before she said, "Please."

Randy didn't have a chance. Even though Travis knew his brother had planned to make her beg even more, the big man caved like a boxer with a glass jaw.

"Hell. I guess so. We'll need to get supplies while we are out. Do you know which one you want?"

She grinned and thrust the runt she was holding out at him. "This one. He needs extra attention, and as small as he is, he isn't getting it with all of the others around."

"Well, put him back and we'll come get him after we get back. He'll be fine till we make it back from town." Randy stood up and waited for her to replace the little thing before he helped her to her feet.

To their surprise, she hugged both of them and thanked them. Then, as if realizing what she'd done, she raced out of the barn. He and his brother looked at each other and shrugged. It was a start. Then

Randy grinned and Travis had a feeling his brother had an idea that would prove to be dirty.

"What?"

"I plan to use that kitten for all it's worth."

"What do you mean?"

"How about a hug for letting her keep that rat you got?"

Travis pretended disgust and stepped back. "Not on your life, man."

Randy just grinned and headed for the barn doors. "I think it will work just fine. Since the cats are my domain, you're going to have to figure out your own trick to getting hugs from our Angel."

Travis couldn't help but chuckle. Leave it to Randy to figure out an underhanded way to get some attention from their woman. Well, two could play at that game. He'd figure out something. He wasn't about to let Randy steal all of her affection right off the bat. Shaking his head, he followed the two back to the house where he watched them load up to head into town. Then he walked back out to the stables and saddled up his horse to check out those cat tracks for himself. He had a lot of planning to do and riding out along their boundaries would be just the place to do it.

Chapter Eleven

Angela had a good time shopping with Randy. It surprised her that he could be so playful when usually he seemed more reserved. When they started picking out vegetables in the produce section, he'd made comments about everything she picked up.

"What about cucumbers, Angela? Do we need nice thick, long ones for anything?" He wiggled an especially large one in her direction.

"Randy. Put that down. We aren't having salad. No cucumbers." She'd felt her face grow hot and quickly turned away from him to examine the tomatoes.

She started feeling them and picking out the firm but ripe ones. Randy wandered over and picked up one. When he squeezed it like she was doing, it squished and he growled. Angela couldn't stop the snort and subsequent laughter that escaped at the disgusted look on his face. She quickly grabbed some paper towels that were on a roll near them and held them out while trying to stop laughing.

"Why is it you can squeeze them but they burst on me?"

"I don't squeeze them as hard as you do."

"I think that one was rotten in the first place. It was all squishy."

"That's why I look for the firm fruit."

"Yeah, that reminds me of a woman's breast. I bet yours are nice and firm with just the right amount of squeezability."

"That's not even a word, Randy. And stop talking about my boobs." She took her tomatoes and pushed her cart toward the cabbage and onions as her face heated up at his suggestive observation.

While she chose the cabbage and onions for the slaw, Randy drifted over to stand in front of the melons. She picked out what she needed then turned to find Randy holding up two cantaloupes in front of his chest. He waggled his eyebrows. Angela couldn't help but laugh at him.

"You're incorrigible. Put those back before you bruise them."

He frowned and looked at them. "You can bruise them like you can a breast?"

She rolled her eyes and took one from him to replace it in the bin.

"Hey, why don't we cut up some fruit for dessert like watermelon and cantaloupe instead of making something? It would save time and be better for us."

"That's actually a good idea."

"Hey, you act like I can't have good ideas." He pouted at her.

Angela laughed. "It's not that I think you can't have them, it's that most of the time you're more interested in how to be bad."

"Well, I'm okay with that." He followed her as she started thumping the different melons before choosing one.

She was surprised when he didn't make any more comments while she picked out a couple of watermelons and several melons as well as some strawberries and peaches. Instead he followed behind her until she got to the meat section. Once there, he took over, talking to the butcher and telling him what they needed. Since he seemed to know what he was doing, she wandered off to grab the hamburger buns they would need.

When she made it back with her arms full, it was to find a very beautiful woman standing much too close to Randy to be just an acquaintance. She stopped in the middle of the aisle and stared as they talked. Randy kept shaking his head. He was pressed between the cooler and the strange woman but he made no move to move to either side. Angela's stomach sank as her heart sped up. Why was she letting this bother her? She had no hold on them. They weren't her men, and she'd been trying to avoid any type of entanglement with them from the beginning.

Still, the sight of the overly affectionate female hanging all over Randy pissed her off. Tears burned the back of her eyes. Before she could stop herself, Angela stomped over to the buggy and dumped the buns in without worrying about whether they got smashed or not.

"Is the meat ready yet, Randy? We need to get back to the ranch. I've got things to do." So what if her voice came out a little bitchy.

The woman looked over at her, giving her the once-over then dismissing her as if she were nothing. That made her even madder. The bitch acted as if she were beneath her or something.

"I've got to go, Belinda. It was nice seeing you again." Randy tried to extract himself from the woman but wasn't having much luck.

"But, Randy, we haven't settled on a date yet."

"I told you, Belinda. I'm busy and don't have time for that. Now move so I can go." He finally moved to the side and lunged for the basket, taking it out of Angela's hands. "Let's go, honey."

She could feel the other woman staring daggers in her back as they made their way to the front of the store. She couldn't help but feel some satisfaction that it was her that Randy was leaving with and not that blonde bimbo with fake nails. The sight of those bloodred nails fiddling with the buttons on Randy's shirt had sent red-hot rage surging through her blood. She'd never felt anything like that before. She wasn't normally a violent person, but she'd itched to scratch that woman's eyes out.

"One more detour, Angela. We need to look over in the pet section and find what you need for the little rat." Randy led her over to that aisle and helped her pick out what she needed.

"Okay, litter pan, litter, kitten food, kitten milk, and a brush. That's the main things. What else do you need?" he asked as he piled everything under the shopping cart.

"I'm going to use one of my old shirts for his blanket and a box for his bed, but he needs a few toys to play with while I'm busy at work."

Randy helped her choose a long feather, a jingle ball, and a small furry mouse. Then they pushed the full cart to the checkout stands. While Randy unloaded the supplies, she arranged them on the belt so that the bag boy would put them in the right bags. She didn't want anything to get ruined just because it was in the wrong bag. She shivered at the thought of the buns ending up with one of the cantaloupes. Not many people knew how to bag groceries, much less teenagers.

She watched the teen bagging their purchases to be sure he didn't mess up while Randy paid for the groceries. To her surprise, the young man seemed to know how to separate out the meat from everything and to put the buns in separate bags from anything heavy. When the kid started to push the cart out for them, Randy gave him a tip and told him he could handle it from there.

"There are women here who need the help more than we do, son." The teenager smiled and nodded his head before heading back to the next register.

Randy helped her up in the cab of the truck before loading the bags into the backseat. Angela went over the grocery list and compared it to their receipt to make sure they hadn't forgotten anything. Then she added up in her head how much she owed Randy for the kitten's supplies.

When she tried to hand him the money, he frowned and pushed her hand away.

"What are you trying to do? Make me mad?"

"I'm paying you back for my kitten's supplies. I don't expect you to pay for my pet."

"Think of it as an, um, welcome-the-new-pet gift," he said as he started the truck.

"It's too much, Randy. If it was just a bag of food or a few toys, that would be one thing, but this is too much." She tried to give it to him again, but he pushed her hand away.

"It's from me *and* Travis."

She waited until he was busy backing up then she tried to stuff it in his jeans pocket. His hand trapped hers against his thigh and she realized that it had her thumb brushing along something that definitely wasn't money on the inside of his thigh. She froze.

"Randy? Can I have my hand back?"

"I haven't decided yet." He looked into her eyes for a few seconds then nodded and released her hand.

Angela jumped back to her side of the truck and pretended to be busy with her purse as Randy drove. God, he felt big. There was no way she could mistake the size of his cock considering where her thumb had been in relation to his crotch. A mild shiver traveled down her spine. She knew her face and neck were red by how hot she felt there.

"You're cute when you blush, honey."

"Don't, Randy."

"Don't what?" She could hear the smile in his voice.

"Tease me. Don't have fun at my expense."

"Angela, I would never do that. I just think you're cute when you get all red and embarrassed. All you did was touch my cock through my jeans. It was an accident. No big deal."

Angela tried to relax and take it like he said as no big deal, but to her it was a big deal. She'd gotten wet thinking about it. Right now, her pussy was soaking her panties and her mouth felt dry. She shouldn't be having these feelings for her bosses. The only place this could lead was to heartbreak and unemployment. She had to get a hold of her hormones and put some distance between herself and the two sexy ranchers or she was doomed. Somehow that didn't make her feel any better. Instead, she felt as if she would choke on all the emotions that threatened to push through.

Neither one of them talked the entire trip back to the ranch. She could only assume that Randy was thinking about the blonde sex bunny from back at the store. Needless to say that thought only made her feel worse. By the time they made it back she was ready to go back to the cabin and hide. Instead, she found herself walking to the barn with Travis to get her kitten.

* * * *

Once back at the cabin with the tiny ball of yellow-and-orange fur, Angela set up the litter box and the kitten's food and water bowls. Then she spent the next thirty minutes showing him where it all was over and over again until she thought he was familiar with the way to get to them.

She planned to fix a salad for dinner and then go to bed early since she would need to be up early to start getting the various side dishes for the cookout ready. After wearing out the ball of fur by playing with all of its toys, she settled it in the box her boots had come in with one of her old shirts and left it sleeping while she fixed her salad.

No matter how hard she tried to not think about Randy and the woman or how his cock had felt against her thumb, she couldn't numb her mind to it. Instead she jumped from one thought to another, getting so angry with herself that she finally let out a frustrated yell. The kitten woke up and immediately started mewing for his family.

Angela bent and picked up the little thing and sat in the chair with it cradled in her arms. He kneaded her chest and purred next to her ear after climbing up to curl up on her shoulder in the curtain of her hair. He needed a name, one he could grow into one day. She considered several before finally settling on Harley Davidson, Harley D for short.

After settling Harley D down for the night once again, Angela took a quick shower and jumped into bed. She had a long day ahead of her and wanted to be sure everything turned out okay. She'd never put together a meal for this many people before other than family get-togethers. Sure, this was just a cookout, but it was important to her bosses for some reason.

Dreams of Randy, Travis, and the blonde bitch tortured her all night. Tossing and turning, she fought her emotions while trying to keep her job in a strange dream world that mirrored her own.

* * * *

"Angela sure was quiet when you got back." Travis watched as Randy put away some of the items from their shopping trip.

"Yeah. I think it was a combination of things."

Travis waited, but Randy didn't seem to be willing to elaborate on his own. Finally he stomped over to the fridge and pulled out two cold beers. Handing one to his brother, he popped the top on his and took a long pull before interrogating his brother.

"What things?"

Randy sighed and opened his can before answering. "Well, on the way back she tried to get me to take her money for the cost of the kitten's things. I refused and she tried to stuff it into my pocket."

"And?" Travis prompted when Randy didn't elaborate.

"I grabbed her hand to stop her, and it trapped her so that her thumb was playing footsie with my cock. I think it embarrassed her."

Travis chuckled. "I'd wager it was harder on you than it was on her."

"Funny. Ha-ha." Randy carried his beer into the living area and collapsed onto his recliner.

"That wouldn't have been enough for her to give us the silent treatment. I was planning on a nice hug or maybe even a little kiss out of helping her with the kitten, but she pretty much shut me down."

"It might have had something to do with her seeing Belinda trying to crawl up my body." Randy sighed and closed his eyes.

"Fuck!" Travis sat down in his recliner and scowled at the floor. "What in the hell is she doing back in town?"

"Hell if I know. She was more interested in trying to get me to come over and see her than I was in asking her why she was back in Riverbend."

"That bitch is trouble with a capital *T*. She better not show her face on the ranch."

Travis wanted to strangle the woman. Only his belief that women should never have to worry about violence kept him from making good on that thought. When they had first bought the ranch over three years ago, she'd convinced them she loved them and wanted to be their woman. Then when things had gotten serious, she had gotten tired of them spending so much time on the ranch when she wanted to go out more. She wanted them to take her to Dallas and Austin to shop or take her out to eat somewhere besides the Riverbend Diner.

It didn't take long before they decided that she didn't really love them. It was their potential money she was in lust with and they were just a means to an end. When she'd realized that Travis was on to her, she tried to convince Randy that they didn't need Travis. She loved Randy more than she did his brother. She had almost put a wedge between them that wouldn't heal. All in all, it had hurt Randy more than it had him because he'd never really fallen for her like Randy had. To this day he blamed the entire ordeal on himself for not picking up on her materialism and putting a stop to things before his brother fell in love with her.

"I know that. I tried to get away from her without making a scene, but Angela walked up with the hamburger buns before I could manage it." He sighed. "The good news is that I think her reaction proves that she cares about us even if she won't admit it."

"The bad news is that women don't like being played. She's not going to like thinking that you're seeing someone while you're flirting with her, Randy."

"I'm not fucking seeing her!" he nearly roared.

"I know that. She won't though."

Randy rubbed his face. "I'll just have to be sure and set the record straight. At least Belinda won't be at the party tomorrow. We can work on Angela then."

"Remember to introduce her to everyone and touch her a lot. Make sure she realizes that we're interested in her even with our friends around so she'll get it out of her head that we just want to fool around with the hired help." Travis turned up the beer and finished it.

"Maybe I should handle the grill while you take her around. She's going to be pissed at me because of Belinda."

"No way. Number one, you always burn the meat and number two, you need to get back in her good graces, fast."

Randy scowled at his brother. "I don't always burn the meat. That was one time."

"Once is enough, little brother."

"Hell. I'm going to bed. We've got to get up early tomorrow. Angela will be over here at the crack of dawn getting things ready for the party. What time is everyone supposed to show up?" Randy asked as he stood up and stretched.

"I told everyone to show up about two. The hands have already pulled all of the picnic tables out around the patio."

"You know, we really should think about adding a pool this year. As hot as it gets, I'm sure Angela would enjoy swimming some, and it would be more fun when we have people over. Remember the party over at Jared and Quade's last year?"

Travis nodded his head. "You're right. We'll talk about it next week."

"I'm heading up. See you in the morning." Randy walked off, leaving his empty beer can on the end table.

Travis stood up and grabbed both of their empties and carried them into the kitchen to toss. He looked around the room and realized how much he enjoyed having Angela working in there beside them. It made their house more like a home. Walking inside at the end of a hard day to the smells of home-cooked meals just felt right to him. Not because there was someone cooking for them, but because Angela was the woman in their kitchen waiting for them.

Somehow he had to figure out how to prevent Belinda from running off the best thing that had ever happened to him and his brother. He had no doubt the bitch would try. She was vindictive as hell and had felt not one iota of remorse for nearly driving a wedge between him and Randy over her. No, she was dangerous, and he would do well to watch out for her.

Nothing was going to come between them and Angela. She was the answer to their prayers in more ways than one. For the first time since Belinda had left, Randy was on the same page as him, and he owed it all to their angel. She was the glue that bound them together.

Chapter Twelve

Early the next morning, Angela began pulling things out of the fridge to cook the guys' breakfast so she could get to work on the fixings for the cookout. She was in a foul mood thanks to very little sleep and disturbing dreams. The one bright spot of waking up that morning had been Harley D's cute antics and heartwarming purrs in her ear.

She had brought him with her, complete with his necessities, and set him up in the office with the door closed. She would check on him periodically throughout the day. The little kitten was too young to leave on his own all day. She didn't think the guys would mind, but at this point, she didn't much care if they did. She was mad at them despite the fact they hadn't really done anything wrong. It had been her dream bosses who'd acted like man whores.

By the time Randy and Travis made it downstairs, she had their breakfast ready. She shooed them away from the kitchen and poured their coffee as they filled their plates.

"What about your plate, Angel?" Travis asked when she didn't sit down with them.

"I've already eaten. I need to get started on the food." She hurried back to the kitchen area, leaving them alone at the table.

"How's the little munchkin this morning?" Randy asked.

She didn't look up. "I named him Harley Davidson, Harley D for short. He's fine. I set him up in the office for now. I'll keep a watch on him.

She could hear the men talking in low murmurs over at the table, but she refused to try and eavesdrop. It was none of her business no matter what it was about. She was their sometimes cook and office manager and nothing more. The sooner she got that through her thick skull, the better off she would be.

While she was cutting up the cabbage for slaw, Randy and Travis walked over and rinsed off their plates before adding them to the dishwasher. Travis hugged her from behind and dropped a kiss on her cheek.

"Thanks, Angel. That was delicious."

Randy moved up and kissed the top of her head. "Sure was, honey. What do you need help with?"

"Nothing. Get out of the kitchen so I can work." Damn, she hadn't meant for her voice to come out so clipped. "Thanks for asking though."

"Angela, we didn't mean for you to handle all of this yourself. We can help." Travis stood so close to her she could smell the clean, fresh scent of his soap and shampoo.

The scent washed over her so fast she had to close her eyes to regain control. What was it about the two brothers that made her want to throw good sense out the window?

"I've got it covered. Why don't you two fill the coolers with ice and start icing down the beer and drinks? That way the ice machine will have time to make more ice by the time your guests arrive."

"Good idea." Randy squeezed her shoulders before walking out of the kitchen. "Get the coolers out of the garage, Travis. I'll meet you around back."

Travis grunted and headed in the other direction toward the front of the house. Once they were both out of range, Angela all but collapsed against the counter. The tension was thick enough to cut with a knife. What was wrong with her? She had to get over this or she'd lose her job for sure.

The rest of the morning was taken up with cooking and fixing the various side dishes they had decided on. She ended up directing them around while taking breaks to check on the kitten. Harley D was doing fine. He easily entertained himself with his toys and napped in between play sessions wherever he fell.

By one, everything was ready and waiting for the guests to arrive. She'd made up several pitchers of tea and lemonade in case anyone didn't want beer or soft drinks. She vaguely remembered that one of the women coming was pregnant. She probably wouldn't want either alcohol or caffeine. Angela hoped the lemonade would be okay.

When everyone started arriving, Randy dragged her out of the kitchen to help him welcome the guests. She felt very uncomfortable as he introduced her as a friend of theirs who also ran their office. Why make her seem like someone more important than she was? What about the woman she thought they had planned to be with them? The next thing she noticed was that the guests arriving were all in ménage relationships.

"There's our favorite accountant," Randy said as two men surrounding a pregnant woman walked through the back gate to where they were having the party.

The pretty auburn-haired woman looked to be a good seven or eight months along. She was about twenty-seven years old with amazing green eyes that sparkled when she answered Randy.

"I'm your only accountant although I heard you finally found someone smart enough to figure out your office mess. Is this her?" She walked over to Angela and held out both of her hands. "I'm Caitlyn. I'm so happy to meet you."

"It's a pleasure to meet you, too. Yes, I'm Angela." She couldn't help but smile back at the lovely woman.

"You have no idea how happy I was to hear that they'd found someone to take over their office. I've been dreading next year's tax season just because of them."

Angela chuckled. Then the woman's two men were scooping her up and carrying her off.

"Come on, baby. You need to be off your feet. You promised to behave if we let you come."

Randy's snicker next to her had her looking over at him. "They are so overprotective it's funny."

"I think it's sweet."

"Caitlyn thinks its bullshit!" the woman in question yelled from across the patio.

"None of that, baby. You don't need to be getting upset."

Angela wasn't sure which of the two men said that, but it had her almost in stitches when the next threesome arrived. Randy shook both of the men's hands then introduced her to all of them.

"Angela, this is Brian, Andy, and Tish. Brian is Caitlyn's brother. They own a shop in town that has some really interesting things in it."

"Oh. You have the new-age store. The lady at The Scent of a Woman said you would have some candles that matched my lotion."

Tish stepped up and shook her hand. "That's right. We make candles with all the same scents as their soaps and lotions."

"I'll be sure to stop by the next time I'm in town." Angela liked Tish right away.

By the time everyone had made it, the party was in full swing. Angela slipped away to check on Harley D then grabbed a glass of lemonade and carried it out to see if Caitlyn wanted it.

"Oh, bless you, Angela. I was sipping on the Sprite, but I really don't like it. This will be perfect."

"You're welcome. I wish I had thought about it and gotten some decaf tea for you."

"Nonsense. This is perfect. I love lemonade. How do you like living out here on the ranch?" she asked.

"I love it. It's so pretty out here. The cabin I'm living in is perfect."

"I hear you're originally from Mississippi. It's probably quite different here in Texas than it is back there."

"You can say that again. I miss some things about living in the Delta, but not much. The wide open spaces out here are so much nicer. Plus there isn't near the amount of humidity we had back there. You felt like you could squeeze water out of your lungs out there."

"What do you think about Randy and Travis?" Caitlyn's eyes watched her men as she asked the question.

"They are really good men. They took a big chance on hiring me like they did. I couldn't ask for better bosses." Angela was pretty sure hearing about their qualities as bosses wasn't what the other woman had in mind.

"Hey, Caitlyn. I came over to see if you needed anything." Tish, the woman's sister-in-law, walked up and took a seat next to her.

"I'm fine. Angela brought me some lemonade to drink."

"Oh! Thank you so much, Angela. I should have thought about that there might not be anything you could drink here, Caity." Tish reached out and rubbed the other woman's belly. "How is my little niece doing in there?"

"Nephew, Tish. It's going to be a boy." One of Caitlyn's men walked up and squeezed his wife's shoulder. "How are you doing, baby?"

"I'm fine! Go away. We're having girl time. You know, the opposite of boy time."

He chuckled and nodded at Angela. "Don't let her fool you. She loves me the most." Then he walked off, leaving Caitlyn growling behind him.

"Sometimes I could knock their heads together," she said.

Angela laughed. "I think it's sweet to have two men treat you so special like that. I can't even imagine it."

Tish and Angela looked at each other and laughed. Before she could ask them what they were laughing about, two more women walked up to join them.

"Hey, Lexie, Bethany, join the crowd." Tish scooted over some so that the other women could sit down.

"You look absolutely wonderful, Caitlyn. I take it the boys are acting like overprotective wolves," Bethany said.

"You hit the nail on the head. Now give me your hammer so I can knock some sense into those two." Caitlyn frowned. "I feel great though. No more nausea and other than some ankle swelling when I'm on my feet too long, I'm not having any other problems."

"That's a blessing." Lexie's long red hair was striking to say the least. It almost glowed in the early May sunshine.

They all talked about what was going on around town the next hour until Travis announced that the meat was ready.

"Oh, goodness. I've neglected my job. It was great talking with all of you. I better get back to work before I get fired." Angela hurried into the kitchen to bring out the side dishes.

To her surprise, all of the other women except for Caitlyn, who Tish said had been sequestered at a table between her men, arrived to help her carry things out. As much as she appreciated their help, she was scared it would look bad for her to allow the guests to help do her job. No matter how many times she told them that she had it under control, they just brushed her off and continued with what they were doing.

Once everything was on the tables and the guests had started filling their plates, Angela sighed and retreated to start cleaning up the kitchen before the leftovers would need to be stored.

"Angela? What are you doing in here? We're waiting on you to fix your plate so we can eat." Travis's voice caught her by surprise, and she nearly dropped the bowl she was drying.

"I'm cleaning up so it will be easier to handle the rest when everyone is finished."

"That can wait. Come and eat." Travis had a frown on his face.

"But, I'm not a guest, Travis. I'm the cook."

When Travis grabbed her by the wrist and dragged her out of the kitchen with a scowl, she wasn't sure what she'd done wrong. Why was he so upset with her? Was it because she'd been talking with the other women for so long? Maybe they naturally thought she was with them and now he was forced to include her. Randy's expression was more puzzled than angry. She didn't know what was going on.

Travis leaned behind her and said something to Randy that she couldn't hear. Then they were both filling her plate with food. A few minutes later, Randy leaned closer to her.

"We're going to have a talk later, honey." It sounded more like a warning than a promise to her. What was going on?

All through the meal, she noticed how they kept touching her and squeezing her shoulder or her thigh. It was making her very uncomfortable. No one seemed to think it was anything out of the ordinary. Maybe it wasn't and she was making a big deal out of it. Maybe the men around Riverbend tended to be the touchy-feely type and she was reading more into it than they actually meant by it.

After everyone had finished eating, they all got up and began clearing away the dishes. The women helped her put everything away while the men gathered up the trash and disposed of it. In almost no time at all the patio and kitchen were clean. She had never experienced anything like it before. Sure, at family get-togethers back home, most of the women tended to help the family clean up, but the men rarely did much more than make sure the grill was taken care of. This was nice.

Just when she had finally relaxed enough to actually enjoy herself with the other threesomes, she looked up to see the blonde from the grocery store walk through the gate onto the patio. She made a beeline for Randy and immediately wrapped herself around him.

"Randy. I'm so sorry I'm late. I got tied up, but I'm here now, baby."

To his credit, he looked a little ill as he tried to disentangle himself from the woman's octopus-like arms.

"What are you doing here, Belinda?" Travis asked as he walked over.

"I'm here with Randy. Didn't he tell you I'm back?" She grinned at Randy. "Shame on you, baby. You didn't tell your brother that we were seeing each other again."

Angela couldn't stop the quick breath she took. Suddenly it was too hot for her out there in the crowd of people. She started to walk toward the kitchen when Tish and Bethany stopped her.

"Don't go. Show her that she has no hold on him, Angela. She's a bitch that nearly tore the brothers apart with her games." Tish stroked her hand up and down Angela's back.

"They aren't my men. I'm their office manager and sometimes cook. I'm not their woman."

"Screw that, Angela. They look at you as if they could eat you up," Bethany said.

"That's just their hormones. You know how men are. I'd be a quick roll in the sack and then I'd be out of a job when they finished with me. I can't afford that."

She started to walk away again but something stopped her. She turned and looked back at Randy. Something in his eyes seemed almost desperate. Maybe she wasn't their woman, but it was obvious that Randy didn't want to have anything to do with this Bethany either. She wouldn't abandon him to the crazy woman.

Angela walked back over to where the blonde bitch was clinging to Randy while Travis argued with her. The men all stood around them, but it was obvious that they didn't know what to do with her without getting physical. Mac Tidwell was the closest and seemed ready to grab her if an opportunity arose. Well, she was going to give him that opportunity. She eyed him and he nodded at her when she lifted any eyebrow. She could count on him.

"Excuse me, but you have your hands on my man. Let go of him."

The other woman looked at her and laughed. "Where in the world did you come from? You sound like some backwoods hillbilly. Go away, little girl."

"You're ignorant as well as rude and stupid. I'm not a hillbilly. They hail from Kentucky and Tennessee. I'm a redneck, and we don't let blonde bimbos manhandle our men where I come from. Let. Go. Of. Him. Now." She stepped closer to the woman despite how much taller she was to Angela's short stature.

"You've got to be kidding me. Randy. Really? You had to go trolling for trailer trash when I left?"

Randy's face finally changed from uncomfortable and a little bit scared to pure angry, but it was too late. Angela had had enough. She grabbed the woman by her hair and jerked her back before punching her in the nose.

Chapter Thirteen

"Fuck!" Mac, who was the sheriff in Riverbend, grabbed Belinda as soon as she let go of Randy to hold her nose even as he laughed.

"She hit me! Arrest her. I want to file charges." Despite her muffled voice it was clear what she was saying.

"I think not, Belinda. Number one, you were trespassing on private property and had been asked to leave several times. Number two, you should know better than to try and take another woman's man. No way am I stepping into Angela's space right now." Mac continued laughing as he and his brother along with Bethany escorted the woman through the gate.

The other women all crowded around Angela telling her how much they admired her for standing up to the bitch. All she felt now was anger that she'd probably lost her job and made the guys mad. Randy walked over to her and pulled her out of the huddle and thanked everyone for coming. He wrapped his arm around her waist and walked with her inside while Travis saw to everyone leaving. It was more than obvious to her how angry Randy was. He was almost shaking with it. She couldn't tell anything from the careful mask he'd donned since she'd hit Belinda. She fought the tears that built behind her eyes. She refused to cry in front of him. Even when he fired her, she wouldn't allow herself the luxury of crying.

Randy didn't stop walking until they had reached the living area. Then he stopped and pointed at the couch.

"Sit. I'll be right back. Don't move from that spot."

She sighed and sank onto the soft cushions, wishing they would swallow her up so that she could avoid the entire confrontation. She wasn't sure how long she sat there, but finally she couldn't handle it anymore. With as much strength as she could gather, Angela stood up and walked to the office where she gathered up Harley D and all of his things. She looked around the office to see if she'd left anything before walking out the door and shuffling back to the cabin.

Once inside, Angela set about packing her things in the duffle bag and a couple of boxes she had accumulated and set it all by the front door. Then she made a phone call, leaving the phone on the counter, and waited. She cuddled Harley D to her chest and wondered what she was going to do now. Why had she punched the woman in the nose? She could have walked away or anything besides hitting her. She wasn't normally a violent person. She'd never hit anyone in her life.

She saw a truck pull up outside the door. She sighed and bent to pick up her bag. When she opened the door, it was to find Randy and Travis standing outside the door. Evidently Homer had called them instead of coming to get her. She just stared at them. Finally, Travis took her bag from her and Randy bent and picked up one of the boxes. Then he returned and grabbed the other box. No one said a word. Travis returned and indicated that she should get into the truck.

She had intended to get in the backseat, but Travis shook his head and opened the front door. She climbed up and put on her seat belt while the men got in and fastened theirs. She stared straight ahead as they pulled out of the drive in front of the cabin and headed down the long drive that led to the road to town. She cuddled Harley D in her arms and tried to keep from touching either man.

No one said anything and after a while, staring out into the dark ahead slowly lulled her into sleep. When she woke up with a start, it was to find that they were stopped in front of the guys' house and they were opening the doors. Harley D was in Travis's arms as he guided her down out of the cab of the truck.

"What's going on? I thought you were taking me to town." Her raspy voice barely registered, but evidently Travis heard her.

"We had no intention of taking you to town and dropping you off somewhere. We were just waiting for you to fall asleep so we could bring you home."

"I don't understand. I thought…"

"That's where you made your first mistake, Angel," Travis said.

"What?" she asked.

"You thought instead of talking to us," Randy added.

"But I punched that bitch in the nose at your house."

Randy cursed and stomped off after slamming the truck door. She jerked at the sound. Travis took her arm, cradling the kitten in his arms before leading her toward the door. When she stepped inside their house, Travis held on to her arm as he walked into the kitchen and then the laundry room where he checked to be sure the back door was locked before he set the kitten down and closed the door to the kitchen.

"Randy will set up Harley's things for him before he comes to bed."

"What?" She shook her head. "I don't understand what is going on."

"Your second mistake was jumping to conclusions when you had no idea what the real situation was."

He started toward the stairs, pulling her behind him as he began to climb them. She'd never been upstairs before. Fear warred with curiosity as they stepped onto the landing.

"Where are you taking me?"

"We have a lot to talk about, Angel. Since we can't trust you to stay put, you're sleeping with us tonight."

"What! I can't sleep with you. I'm your office manager."

"Well, as far as I can see, you quit when you walked out and called our foreman to take you to town. So technically, you're not sleeping with your bosses now."

He pulled her down the long hall past several doors to where a set of double doors opened into a massive bedroom. He flipped on some lights and the true beauty of the room emerged from the shadows. Warm, polished oak floors gleamed in the light with plush throw rugs on both sides of the huge bed that sat in the middle of the room. The bedcovers had already been thrown back on the bed as if waiting for someone to climb in.

Travis pulled her over to where a love seat with two plush chairs formed an intimate sitting area with side tables between the chairs. He pointed at the love seat.

"Sit down. We'll wait for Randy. We need to get some things straight."

Angela sat down on the love seat and looked around the room. Her attention was snagged from the sight of two chests of drawers sitting on either side of the room and the gorgeous dresser across from the bed to where Travis was pulling off his shirt.

She'd seen both men without their shirts on several occasions when they came in and stripped them off in the laundry room due to some mishap. Still, the sight of all that bare skin stretched tight over hard muscles took her breath. Her hands itched to explore his broad shoulders and trace each bulge. She wanted to lick her way from nipple to nipple and follow the path of light brown hair down to where it disappeared beneath the waistband of his jeans.

His fingers unfastened the top button of his jeans before he sat in one of the chairs across from her. She looked away when his eyes caught her staring at where that button was open. Heat crept up her neck and face to have been caught looking.

Just when she thought she would go crazy with the silence, the sound of someone climbing the stairs caught her attention. Randy walked sock-footed into the room. He immediately removed his shirt, dropping it on the floor as he walked over to the empty chair next to his brother. He, too, unfastened the top button of his jeans before sitting down.

"Now that Randy is here, we need to talk, Angel. Why did you leave?"

"Because I couldn't bear to have you fire me." She didn't look up from where she had her hands tightly clasped.

"Why did you think we were going to fire you?" Randy asked.

"Because I hit your…"

"Don't you dare call that woman my girlfriend. She's not my fucking girlfriend!" Randy yelled.

"I wasn't going to say girlfriend. I assumed you invited her and that she was still a friend," she said, quickly dropping her gaze once again.

"I didn't invite her! She just showed up. Someone must have mentioned that we were having a cookout and she invited herself." Randy wiped both hands over his face. "She's nothing to me, honey."

"Then why did you let her hang all over you?" she asked.

"That's on me, honey. I was being stupid. I never should have let her touch me, but I wasn't thinking straight. I won't lie to you. She used to be our girlfriend, but she tried to pit us against each other and we broke it off."

Angela looked from him to Travis then back again. "You loved her?"

"I–I thought I did once. But I know it was purely lust and sex now. She means nothing to me, Angel. I promise."

"It doesn't matter. You don't owe me anything. I was just your office manager. I had no right to interfere, and hitting her like I did was wrong." She shook her head and returned her gaze to her hands once again.

"Angela, you mean more to us than just our office manager. Surely you know that." Travis sounded as if he was choking.

She looked up. "Well, yeah. I cook for you, too. But I still shouldn't have acted like I did."

"I can't believe it. We're going to have to spell it out to her, Travis." Randy stood up and paced beside the chairs. "She still doesn't get it."

"Get what?" she asked.

What where they trying to tell her? Nothing made sense anymore, and she was so tired. She just wanted to lie down somewhere and go to sleep. She had no doubt that depression over losing her job and any friendship with Randy and Travis was sinking in.

Randy stopped next to her and knelt down so that when she looked up, he was almost at eye level. He clasped her hands in his and squeezed them.

"Angela. We love you. We intended to court you until you fell in love with us as well, but things have changed. We don't want to lose you, honey, so we're just going to be honest with you. We want you to be our wife."

Before she could say anything Travis knelt on the other side of her and held out a small box in his hand. Randy let go of her hands and turned them over so that Travis could place the box in them.

"What is this?" she asked in a trembling voice.

"Open it up, Angel," Travis said.

She slowly opened the box and gasped. Inside was the most gorgeous ring she'd ever seen. A solitaire diamond that had to be two carats sat nestled between two sapphires that gave depth and color to the center stone. She'd never imagined anything so beautiful before. Looking up she tried to see what they were trying to tell her. Surely they didn't mean what she thought this meant.

"The sapphires match your lovely eyes. We bought this ring the day we took you shopping that first time." Travis took the box from her hands and pulled out the ring. "Angela, would you marry us? We promise to love you and take care of you forever."

Randy touched her cheek with his hand. "I love you, honey. We will protect you and do everything in our power to make you happy. Please don't say no."

"We thought to give you some time to get to know us before we asked you, but the more we tried to get close to you, the harder you pushed us away. You were so set on not sleeping with your bosses that you refused to see that we loved you for you." Travis held up the ring once more. "Please let us prove to you how much we love you. Wear our ring and be our woman."

Angela couldn't believe what they were saying. They really wanted her to be their wife. They weren't just trying to get her to have sex with them. They were serious about her, serious about their feelings for her. She couldn't speak around the tears clogging her throat. How could they love her? She was nobody, a Mississippi hick with nothing to her name.

Looking into their faces, she saw love in their eyes. She knew without a doubt that she loved them. She had been fighting it, but she knew she had failed. Now, seeing them on their knees before her asking her to marry them, Angela wanted that more than she wanted anything else. She nodded her head and smiled at them.

Travis quickly slipped the ring on her finger and kissed it before pulling her into his arms and mating her mouth with his. She melted in his arms and was thankful that Randy stepped in behind her to help hold her up. Then he got in on the action and kissed her cheek and behind her ear before sucking on her earlobe.

"I've got to have you, Angel. Will you let us make love to you?" Travis asked.

"I want you, too. Both of you," she said in a trembling voice.

Travis picked her up and carried her over to the bed. He carefully set her down, making sure she was steady on her feet before they began to strip her of her clothes. By the time she was standing in her bra and panties next to the bed, she was a melting mass of heat that needed them more than she needed her next breath.

"Fuck, her panties are soaked, Travis." Randy was on his knees once more as he pulled her underwear down.

He had already removed her boot socks along with her boots earlier. Now he lifted her panties to his nose and inhaled before dropping them to the floor and burying his face between her legs. She shrieked and tried to close her legs even tighter.

"Don't, Angel. Let him taste you. Randy loves eating pussy. There's nothing he enjoys more than licking sweet pussy juice right from the source." Travis's dirty words turned her on more than she would have imagined.

Travis unfastened her bra and released her breasts that were heavy with need. Her nipples had hardened to the point of pain when he ran his thumbs over the tight peeks. When he leaned over and ran his tongue across first one and then the other, Angela nearly lost the ability to remain upright.

"Up on the bed, Travis. I want to spread her wide. I can't get to her like this." Randy pulled back and waited while his brother picked her up.

Angela clung to Travis, marveling at the sensation of skin against skin. She loved the feel of it beneath her hands. Then he settled her back in the middle of the bed and Randy climbed between her legs, pushing them as far apart as he could get them.

"Ah, hell, Travis. Look at how pretty this pussy is."

Travis stood behind his brother and smiled down at her. "It's the prettiest one I've ever seen. How does she taste, brother?"

Randy leaned in and lapped at her pussy juices. "Better than the finest wine. I could make a meal off of her and never be satisfied that I've had enough."

Randy returned to devouring her juices as Travis climbed on the bed and buried his face between her breasts. He licked one nipple while rubbing the other one between his finger and thumb. After a while, he switched sides, as if to make sure they received equal treatment. He licked and sucked each of them then moved higher to capture her mouth with his. The more she moaned, the deeper he took the kiss until she felt as if he was eating her alive.

Pleasure built deep inside her cunt as both men filled her with their love. As Randy slowly built the pressure to come with his mouth and fingers, Travis increased the sensations by pinching and pulling on her nipples. Soon she was writhing between them. When Randy pulled her clit between his teeth and stroked some special spot deep inside of her with his finger, Travis pinched her nipples and demanded that she come.

"Let us have it, Angel. We want to hear you scream for us."

She did. She couldn't have stopped it if she'd tried. Wave after wave of delicious sensation poured over her and inside of her until she thought she would pass out from the intensity of it. When she finally came back to herself and could speak around the panting, she grabbed a handful of their hair in each hand.

"That was amazing. Oh, my God, I've never come like that before."

"We're going to top that, honey," Randy said as he slowly climbed up her body.

He rolled over, pulling her with him. She found herself straddling his waist, the hard thickness of his cock pressed tightly against her clit. She couldn't stop the shiver of awareness that poured over her at the feel of his thick cock. When had he pulled off his jeans?

"Put me inside of you, honey. I want to feel your hot cunt squeezing me."

Angela lifted up and grasped Randy's thick dick and slowly lowered herself onto him. He filled her in a way no one had ever filled her before. His massive shaft touched places that had never been touched before. Randy's hissed-out breath told her that he was feeling the tightness just like she was.

"Aw, hell. You're killing me, Angela. Go easy, baby. You're so damn tight. I don't want to hurt you."

She couldn't stand it any longer. She needed to feel all of him inside of her. She pulled up then slammed back down on him all the way.

Chapter Fourteen

Her hissed-out *yes* could barely be heard over Randy's roar. He grasped her hips and held her still as he panted below her.

"Are you all right?" Travis asked from behind her.

"Mmm. Better than all right. Move, Randy. Fuck me. I need you to fuck me hard."

"Shh, honey. I will in a minute." Randy wrapped his arms around her and pulled her down to his chest.

Travis stared in wonder at her ass. It was so pretty and round. He ran his hand from the curve of her ass up the middle of her spine and back down again. She was beautiful. He could hardly believe she was all theirs.

"Angel, have you ever had anyone in this tight ass before?"

"Hmm?"

"Has anyone ever taken you in your ass before?" he asked again.

"Um, no. I've played around some, but I've never had anal sex." She looked over her shoulder at him.

He didn't see disgust or abject fear in her eyes, only mild curiosity and caution. He relaxed and kissed her hip.

"Will you trust me to take you there? I'll make sure you're ready first, Angel."

She smiled. "Okay. I trust you."

"Just lie there on Randy and let me prepare you."

He stepped away and grabbed the lube out of the drawer in the bedside table. When he stepped back, it was to find his brother whispering to her while he held her ass cheeks apart for him. He and Randy exchanged glances. He knew his brother was warning him to be careful of her. Travis would never hurt her if he could possibly prevent it.

After drizzling the lube around her puckered back hole, he inserted the tip of one finger and slowly pushed it in and out a little at a time.

"That's it, honey. Relax and let Travis get you ready so we can both be inside of you at the same time." Randy's voice held just a hint of waver in it. No doubt he was hanging on to his arousal by a thread.

Travis pressed deeper with his lubed finger and slowly breached her anus. Over and over he pushed in and out until he had no trouble with one finger. He pulled out and added more lube before pressing two fingers together to widen her some.

"Push out, Angela. Relax and press against me. That's it." His fingers slowly sank into her back hole until he was all the way in to the webbing at his hand.

Again and again, he pumped them in and out of her, spreading them to widen her dark passage. By the time she was taking three fingers, he knew she was ready. He nodded at his brother who once again whispered naughty words as he added still more lube to her ass before slipping on a condom and adding lube to it as well.

Travis pressed against the tiny dark rosette with the head of his penis and slowly inched his way inside of her. The pressure around his dick soon had him cursing as he struggled to remain in control and resist the need to plunge deep.

"Easy, honey. Push out and relax. Let him in, Angela. He's going to love you so good. We both are," Randy said.

Travis slowly pressed past the tight, resistant rings until his cockhead popped through. Then the rest of him sank deep inside of her until he was balls-deep in her ass. He'd never felt anything like the tight heat that enveloped him.

"Are you okay, Angela?" he asked through gritted teeth.

"Oh, God. You're inside of me." Her voice sounded strained.

"Am I hurting you, Angela? Tell me, honey. I don't want to hurt you." Worry tightened his stomach.

"No. I'll be okay if you move. I can't stand it. You've got to move, Travis. Randy. It's too much."

Travis sighed in relief and slowly pulled out. Then he pressed back inside of her as his brother pulled out. There was no way he would ever last long enough as tight as she was. He gritted his teeth and concentrated on holding back the explosion he knew was just around the corner. This was pure pleasure and perfect harmony to be inside his woman at the same time as his brother. They were truly bound together even more so than a simple wedding ceremony could ever hope to accomplish.

"Please! Faster!" Angela yelled.

He growled but increased the pace, knowing it meant he wouldn't be able to hold off his orgasm for long. He reached between them and located Angela's clit. As they pounded into her with their cocks, he rubbed at her clit with a finger to bring her along with them. He wanted to be sure she was taken care of before they lost their ability to hold off.

When she climaxed between them, she dragged them along with her as she squeezed them inside her body like thousands of tiny vises tightening along their shafts. Travis felt as if his balls turned inside out as hard as he came. His brother's shout of release sounded just as tortured as his had been. He fought to keep from collapsing on top of them, but his legs wouldn't hold him up any longer. He took them to the bed on their sides. All he could hear over the roaring in his ears was the sound of his heartbeat.

After several long seconds, Travis slowly withdrew from Angela and staggered to the bathroom to dispose of the condom and get a wet cloth to clean up their woman. He carefully wiped her clean then helped Randy move her off of him before he crawled back into the bed and pulled the covers over them.

This was what they had longed for all these years. Not just a woman or someone to sleep with, but a home filled with love and excitement. Angela was their angel in disguise. Had he known when he'd stopped to check out the moving bag on the side of the road that day that he would be meeting his destiny, he would have gotten there faster to keep her from waiting so long in the rain for him. She completed them in a way nothing else ever could. He kissed her cheek and rested his hand on her belly as he slowly drifted off to sleep.

* * * *

Angela smiled as the men on either side of her began to snore. The sound of their soft breathing reassured her that they were there with her and not a figment of her imagination or one of her lustful dreams. If someone had told her that she would find true love on the side of a road, she would have laughed at them.

Instead, she'd found two men who filled her with such love and joy that she couldn't settle down to sleep. All she could do was bask in the wonder of belonging to them. They loved her. It slowly sank in as she cuddled between them. That a redneck girl from a little town in Mississippi could find true love with men like these was a miracle to her.

Travis was always calling her their angel. Maybe it was really them who were hers. They had saved her from the possibility of so many things with their kindness. She would treasure them and the gift of their hearts forever. If it took a lifetime, she would make sure they never doubted her love.

She slowly let the knowledge that they loved her and truly wanted her with them for the rest of their lives sink into her heart. Even now, with their ring on her finger and having heard them tell her they loved her, doubts threatened to snatch her happiness away. How could she ever hope to live up to their standards? They were successful ranchers who knew how to hold their own in any situation. She didn't know how to be anything more than who she was. She had no social skills other than what she'd learned along the way of growing up.

The longer she lay there worrying, the more nervous she became. The thought of disappointing her men upset her to the point that she thought she would start crying at any minute. She didn't want them to know how anxious she was about becoming their wife.

Careful not to awaken them, Angela slipped from the bed. She eased out of the room and down the stairs where she hurried to the kitchen. Tears threatened to escape as she poured herself a glass of water and sat at the bar to try and regain control of her riotous thoughts. Maybe she could spend all of her time in the office and kitchen and avoid meeting too many of their friends.

Almost as soon as that thought came, she dismissed it. They would never allow that. They would expect her at their sides. She'd done okay at the cookout, hadn't she? Maybe she was worrying for no reason. Maybe she didn't need special social skills. The beat of her heart slowly settled until she felt as if she could breathe normally again. After a few more sips of her water, she decided to check on the kitten. The poor thing was just a baby and not used to being all alone for long periods of time.

Angela eased open the laundry room door and smiled to see the little ball of fur curled up in her sleep shirt in his box. It seemed that Harley D acclimated to strange places much easier than she did. She relaxed and softly closed the door. She needed to go back to bed, too. The guys would soon miss her if she didn't. When she turned around, it was to find both men standing in the doorway with their arms crossed.

"Oh. You startled me."

"What are you doing up, Angel?" Travis asked.

"Looks like she was checking on the little rat." Randy shook his head. "The kitten is fine, Angela."

"I know. I wanted something to drink and thought I would see if he was sleeping okay or not." Angela knew it sounded weak by the looks on their faces.

"Naw, something has you upset. I can tell by how your shoulders are set. You're all tense." Travis walked over and gently massaged her shoulders. "We didn't hurt you, did we?"

"No! No, not at all. It was wonderful. I guess I'm just nervous for some reason."

"There's no reason to be nervous, honey." Randy walked up on the other side of Travis and kissed her gently on the cheek. "What has you worrying so much?"

"I don't know. This is all so sudden, and I'm not really the type of woman you're used to."

"What the hell does that mean?" Travis asked.

"What type of woman do you think we're used to?" Randy's voice took on an almost sullen tone.

"I don't know. Someone more like that Belinda woman." She knew she'd said the wrong thing by the frosty look that fell over Randy's features.

"Why are you bringing her up?" Travis asked, frowning.

"She's nothing to us, Angela. We told you that." He stomped over to the window and stared out into the darkness.

Angela knew she'd hurt him but hadn't meant to. She wrung her hands and tried to figure out how to explain to them what worried her. How could she make them understand that she no matter how hard she tried that she was afraid she would never fit into their world. They came from money even though they worked the ranch themselves. They knew the right things to do and say around other people with money. She didn't. She was so afraid she would embarrass them one day.

"I don't know how to explain it to you. I'm scared I'm not going to be able to keep you happy. I've never dressed up like the women around here seem to dress. All I've ever worn has been jeans and T-shirts. Your friends are real nice people. What if I say or do the wrong thing around them?" Angela couldn't stop the sob that broke through. "Everyone is going to think I tricked you into marrying me."

"Why would you think that? Has anyone said anything to you?" Travis pulled her hands away from her face and tipped her chin up. "Why would you think we like fancy clothes and parties? We run a ranch and end up knee deep in manure and mud some days."

"No one's said anything," she said quickly. "But I work for you, and I'm just a country bumpkin from Mississippi."

"So the hell what? We don't want you because you're some rich social butterfly or something. We love you for who you are, Angela, the sweet, kind woman who is as stubborn as the day is long." Randy sighed and ran a hand through his hair.

"We don't care about social graces and could care less about impressing anyone. We're just cowboys, Angel. We may be doing okay right now, but we've been flat broke struggling to keep the cows and horses fed, and if we have some bad weather or the price of beef falls, we could be in a bad way again. That doesn't change the fact that we love you—all of you, inside and out." Travis leaned down and kissed her.

Angela sank into him, letting him take away some of the doubt and fear that plagued her. She soaked up the love and warmth he offered that only increased when Randy pressed at her back and nuzzled the back of her neck as he lifted her hair. Here was where she felt safe and loved. This was what gave her hope and confidence that she could be everything they needed. She gave all of herself back to them in hopes that it would be enough. When they slowly pulled away, she knew the doubt and fear would be back despite their assurances that they wouldn't change their mind about how they felt about her.

Travis picked her up and carried her back through the living room and up the stairs to the bedroom. Randy followed and peeled off his pants as soon as they entered the room. When Travis let her slowly slide down his torso to stand beside the bed, Randy was reaching to remove her top while his brother stepped out of his jeans. As soon as she was naked, they settled her in the bed on her stomach. She lay there wondering what they were planning to do but didn't have long to wait. One of them began massaging her shoulders while the other started at her feet.

By the time they had reached her waist Angela was almost asleep, her worries temporarily subdued by their warm assurances and gentle touches. As they snuggled up to her, she promised herself she would do her best to take care of them and make them happy. Somehow, that would have to be enough.

Chapter Fifteen

Over the next few days, Angela felt as if she were in a cloud. Everything seemed almost surreal with how Travis and Randy kept touching her and telling her they loved her. She felt like a princess who'd woken up from a long sleep. All of a sudden everything was perfect, and she was so scared it would fade away if she wasn't careful.

That morning, Randy brought up her moving in with them. She wanted to but worried about how it would look if she lived with them before they were married.

Travis laughed. "You're not living in Mississippi anymore, Angel. No one is going to think any less of you for living with us."

"Besides, technically, you're already living on our land, so what is the difference?" Randy asked as he spooned eggs onto his plate.

"I guess I'm just old-fashioned and being silly."

"And I love you that way. Are you going to town today?" Travis asked.

"I planned to if one of you could take me," she said, smiling at the guys.

"We've got someone coming to look at a couple of our horses, honey. You can take one of the trucks, though." Randy stood up and walked over to the door leading into the laundry room.

"Get the blue truck's keys, Randy. I know it will get her there and back safely." Travis reached over and squeezed her knee.

Randy returned with a keychain that held two keys on it. "It's parked by the horse barn. You shouldn't have any trouble driving it, honey."

"Oh, and call us when you're almost home so we can come unload the groceries for you. Don't forget to let them load your groceries for you. I don't want you lifting anything heavy, Angel," Travis said.

"I'll be fine. I can handle a little shopping by myself." She smiled.

It felt so good to have someone care about her enough to worry. She didn't want them to worry, but the thought counted. As they finished up breakfast, she mentally went over her list, trying to decide if she had forgotten anything. She planned to make a quick stop in on a few of the shops as well as the grocery. She would start with picking up office supplies then the specialty stores followed by the grocery.

"Angela? Angela!"

She jerked when she realized Travis had been calling her name.

"I'm sorry, what?"

Randy laughed. "She's already daydreaming about the wedding."

Heat raced up her neck that she hadn't been thinking about it. Instead, the thought of planning one scared her to death.

"I–I was just thinking about what I needed to get in town. What did I miss?" she asked.

"We were talking about moving your things over tomorrow. What do you think?" Randy asked watching her closely.

"Oh. Um, can we wait until the weekend? That way I'll have plenty of time to get my things together and it won't take that long."

Travis and Randy exchanged glances. Randy frowned but nodded his head.

"If you want to wait a few more days then I guess so."

Travis smiled and stood up. "What are you doing with Harley D while you're gone to town?"

"I left him at the cabin today. I'll pick him up when I get home this afternoon." She stopped and looked at both men. "Um, do you mind if I have lunch at the diner? I was hoping to look at a couple of stores while I was there."

"Of course not. Enjoy yourself, Angel. Just be home before dark and keep your phone close so we can reach you." Travis rinsed off his plate and stuck it in the dishwasher.

Randy got up with his plate but stopped to kiss her before he stepped aside for Travis to do the same. She loved their kisses. She would never get used to them. When both men had said good-bye and left, Angela gathered the rest of the dishes and rinsed them before adding them to the dishwasher and turning it on.

She pulled out her list and check one more time that she had everything on it. Then she hurried over to the barn to get the truck. The blue truck turned out to be a midsized one that she felt comfortable driving. It wasn't new, but looked in good shape to her. She stopped by the cabin to make sure Harley D was doing okay then drove toward town.

Being on her own for the first time in a long time was nice, though she missed her men. Still, she looked forward to exploring some while she was out. The drive to town didn't take as long as she had expected, but she blamed the pleasant day and interesting sights for it. It was obvious that spring was in full bloom and nearing the summertime mark. Already the afternoons tended to be quite warm. The last several days both men had come inside shirtless at dinner time. She had thoroughly enjoyed the sight and wasn't complaining one bit.

Angela pulled into the outskirts of town and turned toward the street that Uniquely Yours was supposed to be on. She found a parking spot not far from the little shop and walked the short block, window-shopping along the way. There were quite a few interesting stores in the area. She couldn't wait to check out more of them.

Stepping into the new-age store, the first thing she noticed was the lack of cheap-looking jewelry and incense burners that had always been popular in these types of stores back home. Here she found handmade candles, clothes, and interesting statues and furniture. As she looked over the candles, a young woman walked over with a broad smile on her face. She instantly recognized her as Tish, Caitlyn's sister-in-law.

"Hey, Angela. It's great to see you again." She pulled her into a hug. "How are you doing?"

"Fine, thanks. You look nice. I love that dress you have on." She thought the dress looked amazing and comfortable all at the same time.

"Thanks. They are so comfortable. We have them over here." Tish led her over to a stand of the flowing dresses. "I'm sure we have your size if you're interested."

Despite not planning to buy more than the candle, Angela found herself totally enchanted by the dresses. She looked through them all until finally picking out a pale yellow and green one she thought was cheerful but not brassy. Tish kept up a steady stream of talk as Angela picked out the candle she wanted.

When she pulled out her money to pay, Tish zeroed in on the ring on her finger.

"Is that an engagement ring?"

"Um, yes. I'm, um, engaged to Travis and Randy." Angela waited for the gasp of disbelief but it didn't happen.

"That's wonderful! I don't know them that well, but everyone thinks highly of them. I know you're excited! When's the wedding?" Tish asked.

"Oh, well we haven't really decided yet."

"You've got all the time in the world to decide. I'm sure they are chomping at the bit to get you tied to them, though. Don't let them talk you out of a nice wedding. Take your time and have what you want."

Tish hugged her again after she handed her purchases to her. Angela had no doubt that she would be calling her friends to spread the news. Having someone else know about it helped to cement it in her mind, but it didn't help much with her insecurity about measuring up to what she thought they would expect. That led to thoughts of their parents coming soon to visit. What would they think of her?

God! To meet their mother and know that she would want to help plan the wedding scared her to death.

"Hey! Are you okay?"

Someone she didn't recognize stood towering over her with a concerned expression on his face. Angela didn't realize she'd stopped in the middle of the sidewalk on her way to the truck. She realized the stranger was holding her bag as well.

"I–I'm fine. I guess I wasn't paying any attention to where I was going."

The tall man didn't look like he believed her. "Are you sure? You're awful pale. Are you by yourself? Do you want me to call someone for you?"

"No, I'm fine. Thanks." She held out her hand for her bag he was holding.

"I'm Deputy Sheriff Jace Vincent. Are you sure I can't call someone for you?" He handed the bag to her, though it was obvious he was reluctant to.

"Thanks, Deputy. I'll be fine." She hurried back to the truck and climbed in with shaking legs.

The supply store was on the next street. If she hadn't needed printer ink so badly, she might have skipped it entirely and gone straight to the grocery store then headed back to the ranch. Instead, she drove to the next street and parked directly in front of the store that carried everything from no-frills jeans to mouse traps. Travis told her that they carried anything she might need for the office. Looking at the front of the building, she had her doubts. It looked more like a junk shop than a department store.

When she stepped inside though, it was much more impressive. Almost as soon as she walked through the door, a teenage male greeted her and asked if he could help her.

"I have a small list of office supplies I need," she told him.

He took her list and led her toward the back of the store. "I'm Josh. I'll help you get all of this in no time. Do you want a case of paper or just a few packages? Bright white or normal white?"

"I'll take a case of the normal printer paper. We don't use it for anything more than reports and lists. I still have some of the better paper for anything else we might need."

They talked about what she had on her list, and he gathered it all up for her. Once she had paid for her purchases, he and another young man carried it out and loaded it in the truck for her. She was pleased to note that she still had an hour to browse before she planned to eat lunch.

Since she felt better, she wanted to look at the lingerie store. Now that she actually had a reason to wear nice things, she wanted something special for Randy and Travis. Almost from the moment she walked in, Angela felt as if she were in heaven. The store seemed to breathe comfort. She decided it had something to do with the candles she saw flickering around the place. The delicious scent was soothing as was the soft beat of the music she could hear in the background.

"Welcome. I'm Adriana. Feel free to look around. If you need anything, just call for me." A pretty woman of about twenty-eight or so with long brown hair and gorgeous brown eyes greeted her as she stepped deeper into the store.

"Thanks. I'm just looking around right now. The things in your window are gorgeous."

"Thank you. Let me know if you need something." Adriana slipped away as Angela started looking at the lacy panty and bra sets in pastel colors.

By the time she'd explored the store, there wasn't much time left before she needed to head to the diner. She knew it would take her awhile at the grocery. Angela swallowed her nervousness at buying such decadent underwear and handed her selections to Adriana.

"These will look lovely on you. You have the prettiest blue eyes I've ever seen."

"Thank you. There are so many pretty things here that it's hard to narrow down my favorites." She giggled nervously.

"No need to narrow anything down. Just come back often." Adriana winked at her. "I see you're wearing an engagement ring. Congratulations. When you have time, come back and pick out some things to put on your bridal wish list for friends to choose as gifts."

"Oh! I hadn't thought of that. That's a good idea." Angela didn't have the heart to tell her that she really didn't know anyone there who would buy something that nice just for her.

When she received her package, it was to find that her purchases had been carefully wrapped in tissue with a soft scented sachet enclosed. Waving bye to Adriana, she hurried back to the truck and stored her package. Then she drove to the Riverbend Diner for lunch. She was surprised at how busy it was on a Wednesday at almost one in the afternoon. Before she even finished parking, her cell phone rang. Angela noted the number to be Randy's. She smiled as she answered it.

"Hi."

"Hey, honey. Are you doing okay?"

"I'm fine. I was just about to get a bite to eat before I head over to the grocery store. Did you think of something else you needed?" she asked.

"No. Just missing you and wanted to check and see how you were doing." Randy sounded as if he were outside by the various sounds in the background.

"Aw, thank you. I miss you, too. It's more fun when you and Travis are with me."

"Even when I make you get a pair of boots?"

Angela couldn't help but laugh at that. "Yeah, even when."

"Go on and get something to eat. Don't want you falling over from hunger. Remember to let us know when you're almost home so we can unload the groceries for you," Randy said.

"I will. I'll see you soon. Bye."

She hit *end* and dropped the phone back in her purse before jumping out of the truck and walking to the diner's door. Before she had a chance to open it though, another pair of hands beat her to it and held it for her. She looked up and found the deputy sheriff from earlier holding it wide for her to enter.

"Thanks." She hurried inside, stumbling as she did.

Deputy Vincent caught her before she fell, holding her for a second until she was steady on her feet again.

"Seems like I'm saying thanks to you a lot today." She tried to make a joke out of it.

"No problem. Are you sure you're okay?" He looked as if he wanted to say something more, but a waitress she'd not seen before hurried over to where they were standing.

"Just grab a seat anywhere. I'll be right with you." The young woman had to be under twenty-one with oddly colored hair and a stud in her nose.

Angela hurried over to a table by the window and took a seat. She picked up the menu by the napkin holder and looked over it while she waited on the waitress. If the special didn't interest her, she decided on the club sandwich. When she looked up, it was to find the deputy staring at her again. She shifted in her seat, uncomfortable with the attention. Then the teenager returned with a glass of water.

"What can I get you to drink?"

"Water is fine. What is the special today?"

"Chicken pot pie." She popped her gum as she waited.

"That sounds good. I'll have that."

"Coming right up."

No sooner had the waitress left than someone took her place. Angela looked up to find Bethany and Lexie smiling down at her. She could tell by their grins that they knew about her engagement.

"Hey. How are you?" she asked.

"We're fine. Can we join you for a few minutes?" Bethany asked.

"Of course."

They took seats across from her, and Lexie immediately held out her hand in a *gimmie* motion. Angela sighed and slid her left hand out for the two women to ooh and ah over her ring. As much as she enjoyed it, a small part of her worried that she was jumping the gun. What if they changed their minds before they actually got married? Was she jinxing herself by being excited?

"It's beautiful! Aren't you excited? Randy and Travis are great men," Bethany said with a huge smile. "Mac and Mason like them and say they are honest as the day is long."

"When is the big day?" Lexie asked.

"Um, well, we haven't set a date yet." Angela felt her stomach roll.

"Of course not. I wasn't thinking. I bet his parents are coming down to meet you. You'll have to set it when everyone will be there. I'm sure their mom will want to help with the planning. You'll love her. She's down to earth." Bethany waved her hand in a dismissive motion. "She'll be a lot of help to you. If you have any trouble out of your men, you can count on her to set them straight for you."

"Oh! We've got to plan the bachelorette party, so give us plenty of warning when you decide the date." Lexie clapped her hands as she and Bethany stood up.

"Party? Wait. I don't need a party." The roll in her stomach turned into a tsunami in no time.

"Of course you have to have a party. It's a tradition. Don't worry about it. We'll take care of everything." Bethany waved as the two women walked away.

"I take it congratulations are in order." Mattie walked over, carrying her order.

"Hi, Mattie. Thanks." She wasn't sure what to say.

"I'd sit and chat, but we're busy for some strange reason. You tell those men of yours I said to treat you right." With that, the older woman hurried back to the counter to ring up a customer.

Angela looked down at the delicious-looking food and wondered if she would be able to eat it after all.

Chapter Sixteen

Randy could tell something was wrong by the way Travis's face tightened as he talked to Angela. He waited until his brother got off the phone and had slipped it back in its holder before he said anything.

"What's wrong?"

Travis grimaced and shook his head looking over where some of the ranch hands were gathered, discussing the day's work. Evidently they would be talking about it later. He didn't like not knowing what was going on, but at least he knew that Angela was safe and nothing life threatening had happened. Still, waiting never had been his strong point.

"Homer, we're going back to the house to unload the groceries for Angela. If you need anything, call us." Travis pulled off his gloves as he walked toward his truck.

Randy followed him and climbed up in the passenger side as he started the truck and threw it into gear. He didn't say anything, just waited for Travis to start talking. It was obvious that he was trying to organize his thoughts. What in the hell had Angela said—or not said to put him in this mood? He wasn't sure he'd ever seen him this upset before. Plus, he didn't know if he was mad or worried.

"Something's wrong," Travis finally spit out. "She didn't sound right over the phone."

"What did she say?"

"That she was on her way back to the ranch and should be there in the next fifteen minutes."

"That's all?" Randy asked.

How had that gotten Travis's tail in a twist? He was normally the easygoing, laid-back one between them.

"Yeah. It's how she said it. Something had to have happened while she was in town. She sounded distracted, like she wasn't really concentrating on what she was saying, and her voice was shaking."

Randy waited for him to say something more. Even though he would be worried that something had upset her with her voice shaking, it still didn't sound like anything to have Travis as on edge as he appeared to be. There had to have been something more in her voice that he couldn't really explain to Randy. Well it wouldn't be long now. He could see the house just ahead, and a plume of dust was already rising through the trees down the drive leading off the main road. That would probably be from the truck Angela was driving.

The second Travis parked the truck, both of them jumped out of the cab and headed toward the end of the drive where Angela would park the truck once she arrived.

"I get that something has Angela upset, but why are you so close to losing it, brother? What aren't you telling me?" Randy stared at Travis's profile as the other man's eyes never left the drive.

"I don't know. It was just something in her voice. I got a bad feeling come over me. I don't get feelings like that a lot."

"Fuck!" Randy didn't like that one bit.

He started to say something but the blue truck emerged from the trees, pulling into the parking area. Travis hurried over to the driver's door and opened it even before Angela had pulled off her seat belt.

"Hey, Angel. How was your trip?" he asked.

If Randy hadn't known better, he wouldn't have been able to tell that his brother was walking a thin line. He waited to see what Angela said, how she sounded.

"Fine. It was fine. I think I got everything," she said.

Randy's gut tightened at the slightly too-high pitch of her voice. Something was definitely wrong. He watched as Travis helped her down. His brother hugged her then handed her over to him.

"Hey, honey. Why don't you go on inside and we'll bring the groceries in so you can unpack them." He hugged her, noting that although she hugged him back, it seemed a bit reluctant at first.

She nodded, shouldered the strap of her purse, and walked up the steps to the porch. He and his brother watched as she opened the door and disappeared inside the house. He ran his hand through his hair and sighed.

"Something definitely has her preoccupied. We can't let her stew over whatever it is, Travis. We need to confront her about it." Randy watched his brother open the back door with a jerk and start pulling bags out.

"I agree. I'm just not sure we're going to be happy with whatever she's got to say."

"Don't go jumping to conclusions just yet. We need to see what she says." He followed Travis in and out of the house over the next few minutes, carrying bags inside and leaving them on the island for Angela to unpack and put away.

As soon as she'd finished stowing the food and putting away the folded bags, she started working on dinner. Randy wasn't sure if it would be better to wait until after dinner to talk to her or get it over with now. By the look on Travis's face, it was going to be now. He walked over to the door leading to the laundry room and leaned against the door facing.

"Did you see anyone you knew while you were out today?" Travis asked as he pulled two beers from the fridge.

"Um, yeah. I saw some of the women I met at the cookout, Bethany, Lexie, and Tish."

When she didn't elaborate, Randy saw Travis's jaw clench. He didn't like picking things out of people. If Angela made him do that, she would soon find out one of his brother's pet peeves.

"So what all did you talk about?" Travis asked.

"Um, I don't know." She hesitated over what she was doing at the stove then continued. "They noticed my ring. Maybe I shouldn't have worn it to town. I hadn't thought about anyone noticing."

"Why wouldn't you wear it to town? We aren't keeping it a secret." Randy hadn't realized he was going to say anything until he'd already nearly shouted at her.

The look on her face when she turned toward him made him wince. Her eyes lowered toward his hands. Randy looked down and sighed. He was clenching one hand into a fist and the other was crushing the beer can.

"I'm sorry for yelling, Angela. I shouldn't have, but I don't understand why you don't seem to want anyone to know that you're engaged to us. Are you ashamed of being with us or something?"

She jerked her head back and forth. "No! I—we hadn't talked about if we were saying anything yet or not, and I wasn't sure if I'd made a mistake by wearing it to town."

Randy felt relief pour over him like cool water on a hot summer day. He glanced toward his brother. Travis looked relieved, but wasn't completely relaxed as yet.

"Honey, we want you to wear our ring all the time. If anyone asks, then tell them the truth. We're getting married," he said.

"As soon as possible," Travis added.

His brother pulled her into his arms and hugged her close. Randy smiled and started to lean in and kiss her from behind when he saw a brief glimpse of fear in her eyes before she closed them. There was still something not quite right. Should he dig deeper now or wait? He hated waiting, but something told him not to push it just yet.

God, don't let me be making a mistake by letting it drop.

* * * *

Angela closed her eyes and let Travis's love warm her. When Randy started to kiss her then stopped, she'd closed her eyes against the disappointment she was sure she would see in them. She'd failed them when she'd hesitated to let their friends know they were getting married. She hadn't counted on them wanting everyone to know right away.

See, that is why I'm the wrong sort of woman for them. I don't know how to act about things like this.

"I need to get back to cooking or we won't have anything to eat tonight." She carefully pulled away from Travis and Randy.

"Angel. All we need is you. We can eat sandwiches later. I missed you today." Travis took her hand and pulled her toward the living room door.

"The stove…"

"Randy. Turn off whatever is on the stove and come on upstairs." Travis shouldered Angela up over his shoulder and headed for the stairs.

"Put me down, Travis. I can walk."

"Nope. I'm carrying you, so settle down before I spank this sweet ass of yours," he said.

She held on to his waist as she bumped against his shoulder as he climbed the stairs. Thank goodness she hadn't eaten much earlier. All the emotional upheaval paired with the bumpy ride up the stairs on Travis's shoulder would have made her sick. When he bent over to let her stand up again, Angela had to hold on to him for a few seconds to regain her equilibrium.

"God, you're so fucking beautiful, Angel. I love how your eyes get all glazed over when you come. I want to watch you almost as much as I want to taste your pussy."

All she could do was moan as his mouth descended to hers. His lips caressed hers at first, with soft butterfly kisses that slowly spread to each corner of her mouth. Then he seemed to grow impatient with the slow approach and pulled back.

"Open to me. Let me in." He took control of the kiss, plunging his tongue into her mouth and mapping every inch until she swore he had it memorized.

Somewhere through the soft haze of pleasure, she realized that Randy was undressing her. How had she missed losing her boots, socks, and pants? It was only now that he tugged them apart in order to pull her shirt over her head that she realized how caught up in Travis's kiss she'd become. He'd become her world for a few seconds where nothing else mattered.

When she would have felt guilty over Randy being left out, he pulled her from Travis's arms and ate his way down her jaw to her throat, where he soon had her whimpering with need. God, how she wanted, wanted him, wanted them deep inside her. She wanted to feel as if she was a part of them and they'd never want to be without her. She groaned, pulling at Randy's shirt with a desperation that bordered on violence. Skin, she needed to feel his skin against hers. She reached back for Travis once more, but he'd dropped to his knees at her feet. Looking down at him, Angela thought she would die at the expression of need on his face when he looked at her pussy.

Raw desire bubbled up from nowhere she had ever known existed before now. She managed to get Randy's shirt off his shoulders so that he could finish removing it, but no matter how hard she tried, she couldn't get the damn belt buckle to release so she could rid him of his jeans.

"Easy, honey. We've got all the time in the world." Randy took over dealing with the belt and soon had his jeans down around his ankles.

"Damn, your boots!" She wanted to scream with frustration.

"I've already taken them off. Calm down, Angela."

She moaned instead of answering him when Travis began pulling her panties down by the elastic with his teeth. Hot breath combined with smooth lips and sharp teeth left her legs shaking and her pussy weeping. She could literally feel it seeping down to her thighs. She'd never been this turned on before.

"Aw, hell, you smell like heaven, Angel. Pick your feet up for me, baby." Travis helped her lift first one then the other foot so he could remove her underwear.

He began licking and nipping his way up her legs. She squirmed between him and Randy, wanting Travis to hurry and reach her throbbing clit. Instead, Randy jerked her attention back to him when he released the clasp of her bra and jerked it off and down her arms to join her panties on the floor. Angela gasped for breath when he covered one breast with his hand and squeezed while drawing the nipple of the other one into his mouth in a quick, hot pull that had her rising to her tiptoes and grabbing onto his head at her breast.

"God, yes!" She fisted his hair in her hands as he raked his teeth over the now-sensitive nipple before moving to the other one.

Travis must have been feeling left out because the next thing she knew, he separated her pussy lips and ran his tongue over her throbbing clit with just enough pressure to suck all of the oxygen out of her lungs at once. Then he licked and pulled on her pussy lips before stroking two fingers as deep as they would go into her cunt, making her scream.

"Bed, Randy. I can't get to her like this." Travis sounded out of breath, or desperate or both.

Randy grunted but released her nipple with a pop before helping Travis to lower her to the bed on her back. Travis had her legs spread wide before she'd even caught her breath. He licked her juices from her inner thighs before returning to torture her pussy with tongue and teeth. There was no way she would last much longer as he slipped his fingers inside her cunt once more.

They tortured her for what seemed like hours, pushing her closer and closer to the edge then easing her back down again only to start the climb all over again. Soon Angela was begging to come. Tears threatened to fall with all the frustration beating at her.

"Please, Travis. I need to come. God, please!" Her head thrashed back and forth as she held on to Randy's hair with one hand and the bedspread with the other.

"What do you think, Randy? Should we let her come now? Personally, I could go on like this for hours. I'll never get enough of her sweet pussy." Travis's raspy voice held a strain she knew had to be almost as frustrating as she felt.

"Come for us, Angela. Let us hear you scream with pleasure, honey." Randy's voice had gone so low she almost couldn't hear him.

Travis latched hold of her clit with his mouth and attacked it with his tongue while stroking her hot spot deep inside her cunt. Randy pulled and pinched her nipples, sending shards of pleasure/pain straight to her already-primed clit. One second she was gasping and struggling to reach for the orgasm that seemed just out of reach and the next she was flying, soaring higher than she'd ever gone before.

It was several long seconds later that she realized she had been screaming their names as she came. Her throat ached from the abuse and need for something to drink. Both men lay next to her stroking her arms and shoulders while whispering how good she was and how much they loved her. She soaked up their attentions but still needed more. She wanted to feel them inside of her. She needed that more intimate connection. She opened her eyes and stared up into their faces as they looked down at her.

"How do you feel, honey?" Randy asked.

His thick cock pressed insistently against her hip. Angela's mouth watered. She looked down the length of him to where the moist smear of pre-cum connected them. Looking back up, she made sure he could see the lust in her eyes.

"Hungry." She licked her lips.

"Fuck!" Randy said, closing his eyes for a second.

Then Travis knelt next to her. "Up on your hands and knees, Angel. I want you to suck Randy's dick while I fuck this sweet pussy."

She scrambled to her hands and knees and looked up as Randy knelt in front of her. When she lowered her head to lick his cock, her hair fell over her face. Randy immediately pulled it back for her and held it as she ran her tongue around the rim of his cockhead. She felt his fist tighten in her hair as she did. She imagined him squeezing his eyes shut as she slowly sucked the spongy head into her mouth. She hummed around him and was rewarded when he laid his other hand against her cheek as she sucked on just the tip of him.

"Yes!" he hissed out.

Angela dipped the tip of her tongue through the slit, the tangy taste of him exploding across her tongue even as his cock pulsed in her mouth from the sensation. Nothing had ever made her feel this powerful before. She reveled in the knowledge that she was able to affect him like this. She, who had very little experience next to these amazing, wonderful men who claimed to love her, was giving him pleasure.

She pulled back and licked him from balls to tip then slowly drew him back, deep into her mouth, until he hit the back of her throat and she could take no more of him. His quick intake of breath told her how good it felt to him. When she swallowed around him still deep inside her mouth, he cursed and flexed his hands, one still holding her hair and the other at her cheek.

"Fuck, that feels so good. Your mouth is dangerous, honey. God, yes. Just like that."

Angela smiled around his dick, her saliva dripping from her mouth as she rubbed her tongue all along the shaft that filled her mouth. She moved one hand up to caress his balls, letting most of her weight rest on her knees and other hand, trusting that Randy would keep her upright.

Already Randy's balls were beginning to tighten in their sac. She massaged them as she began to milk his cock with her mouth. His heavy breathing and the grunting noises he made confirmed that he was close to losing control. She wanted to make him lose that control.

Though Travis was behind her standing at the edge of the bed caressing her ass cheeks and lower back, he didn't interfere or pull her attentions away from his brother. His occasional comment of how beautiful she looked sucking Randy's cock and how proud he was of how she was doing, only added fuel to her desire to make Randy fill her mouth with his cum. She wanted that part of him.

She scraped her teeth lightly across his cock on the next upstroke and knew she'd finally broken his control when he grasped her head with both hands, digging his nails into her scalp. He didn't hold her head still while he fucked her mouth, but did keep a tight grip as he pumped his hips and she sucked on his cock. With a hoarse shout, he erupted into her mouth, filling her with streams of tangy cum that she struggled to swallow.

Randy collapsed to his side, pulling his spent dick from her mouth. Angela licked her lips clean, satisfied to see his tortured expression when she did. He gasped for breath for a few seconds then moved over toward her and smoothed his hand over her cheek before kissing her.

"That was amazing, Angela. You are amazing. Love you, honey."

She smiled and rested her forehead against his for all of two seconds. Then Travis drove into her from behind in one quick thrust that took her breath.

Chapter Seventeen

"Ah, hell! You're so fucking tight," Travis gasped out. "Hot, wet, and perfect."

Angela dropped her head to the bed and gasped for breath. He filled her to bursting with his thick cock. Randy might have been a bit longer than him, but he was broader. Even as wet as she'd been after her orgasm and sucking Randy, Travis hadn't had an easy time entering her. Every nerve ending in her cunt was on fire, but the friction was delicious, edging her body toward another orgasm. Surely she wouldn't have another one so soon.

Travis gripped her hips as he slowly pumped his dick in and out of her pussy. Each thrust grew harder and faster as she took him deep inside of her. She could feel her climax building in her blood stream and with each beat of her heart. Desperate for more, Angela met each of Travis's thrusts with a backward thrust of her own.

"Faster, Travis!" She wanted to scream at him to pick up the damn pace.

He squeezed her ass cheeks then spread them wide as he continued to shaft in and out of her needy cunt slower than she wanted. When he pressed a finger against her tight anal opening, all she could do was hiss with need.

The feel of his finger pushing deeper into her back hole seemed to break something inside of her. Angela growled and glared at Travis over her shoulder. Why wasn't he fucking her like he meant it? She needed harder and faster to come.

Just when she started to scream at him, Randy surprised her by pulling on both nipples at once, electrifying her body all over again.

The breath left her lungs in a *whoosh* that sounded loud in her own ears. Every nerve ending in her body seemed to be on edge, waiting for the next sensation that would surely take her over the edge and into bliss.

"Fuck me, Travis! Oh, God, I need you harder." Angela's demand came out on a half sob.

As if that was all he had been waiting for, Travis sped up, ramming into her pussy almost as if his cock was a battering ram. Each plunge of his hard dick scooted her across the bed until Randy's body stopped her from moving to the edge. Even as he held her in place, he rolled and pinched her nipples until she couldn't tell where the pain left off and the pleasure took over. Every place they touched thrilled with excitement like live electricity, jumping from nerve to nerve up and down her body.

Travis kept that sneaky finger pumping in and out of her ass in time with each lunge of his hips, burying his shaft deep inside her cunt. The pressure built until her ears were ringing with it.

With no warning, Angela's orgasm sucked her into a whirlwind of pleasure, stealing her breath and ability to scream. Every muscle in her body quivered as they tightened to knots. When everything came rushing back into focus she collapsed on the bed face-first, her arms nothing more than limp spaghetti noodles. If it hadn't been for Travis's cock and the finger still lodged in her ass, she would have been ready for bed.

Somewhere during her blissful climax, Travis must have finished as well because she felt the combined evidence of their pleasure running down her leg. Considering the magnitude of her own orgasm, it was no wonder she hadn't been aware when he had reached his. Even now, she wasn't exactly sure what was going on around her. Everything felt dulled, moving in slow motion.

"Angel? You okay, baby?" Travis's husky voice drew a smile from her.

"Um, hmm."

He chuckled and slowly pulled from her spent body. "Hell, I'm done for. I've never felt anything like that, Angel. You're fucking amazing."

She couldn't do anything more than smile when he kissed the base of her spine. She felt the bed dip, and then several minutes later a warm, wet cloth began cleaning their mess. She didn't even bother to protest this time. She just didn't have the energy.

Randy slowly slipped from in front of her and eased her down in the bed before climbing in next to her. She could hear the two men talking but couldn't make out what they were saying. Then one of them pulled the sheet up over her and she snuggled into Randy's warm body before drifting off to sleep.

* * * *

Travis watched as the woman he loved more than anything else in the world snuggled into his brother's arms and drifted off to sleep. He could still feel her body clamp down around his cock and taste her essence on his tongue. A shiver ran down his spine at the way she'd managed to rock his world in such a short time. He should be the happiest man alive right then. Instead, he was scared, scared that she was keeping something important from them.

Randy nodded while stroking Angela when Travis whispered that he was going to take a shower. Turning away, he shuffled into the bathroom and closed the door. Leaning on the counter, he hung his head as the worry returned full force pushing aside the euphoria of making love with Angela.

"What are you keeping from us, Angel?" Shaking his head, Travis pushed off of the counter and walked over to the shower to turn on the water and adjust it to a temperature just below scalding.

He stepped into the punishing spray of the water and let it pour over him as he tried to settle inside himself. He wasn't about to let anything take away what he and his brother had finally found. It had taken nothing short of a miracle for Randy to put their past relationship behind them and take a chance on Angela. He'd be damned if anything stood in their way this time. Somehow he had to get her to feel comfortable enough to be open with them now. If she kept things from them now, it would only get worse as time went by.

The longer he stood there thinking about it, the more convinced he became that something had happened while she'd been in town. He needed to get to the bottom of it and make sure that Angela knew she could talk to them about anything. How he was going to do that, Travis didn't know, but he was going to figure it out.

As the water began to cool, he quickly washed off and climbed out. After drying off, he turned off the bathroom light and slipped back into the bedroom. When he eased into bed on the other side of Angela, she turned in her sleep to wrap an arm across his chest. Though it went a long way to soothing some of the worry weighing him down, it didn't completely alleviate it. When he finally fell asleep, it was to dreams of losing her.

* * * *

Angela woke early the next morning to find that both men had already gotten up and dressed. She eyed the clock by the bed to find it was only around five in the morning. Why had they gotten up so early? Had something happened on the ranch? Then the fact that she'd left poor Harley D back at the cabin all by himself spurred her into action.

She jumped out of bed and nearly fell on her face, having forgotten how tall the bed was. She quickly rounded up her clothes and did a quick cleanup in the bathroom before dressing and hurrying downstairs. When she couldn't find either man in the house, she decided to go back to the cabin to shower and dress. Walking through the living room, Angela was relieved to find a note taped to the front door. Grabbing it, she read it and relaxed.

Morning, beautiful. We figured you would head to the cabin to change and check on the rat before work. We really need to talk about moving your things to the house. Mom and Dad will be here this weekend sometime. They can't wait to meet you. We had to leave early to move some cattle. See you at lunch. Love, T and R.

Tears welled up in her eyes at how obvious it was that they loved her. She shouldn't feel so insecure when they gave her no reason to doubt how they felt. She vowed to stop letting her own fears rob her of the happiness she had within her grasp. They knew all about her. She'd kept nothing from them about her past. All she had to do was return their love and trust them to keep their word.

Angela held the note to her chest and hurried out the door toward the cabin. When she opened the door, it was to be attacked by a hyper-vigilant ball of fur. Laughing, she cradled the tiny kitten in her arms and talked to him while she quickly tended to his litter box, food dish, and water bowl. Then she plopped him down in front of his meal and escaped to the bedroom. She needed to shower and dress before he lost interest in eating.

By the time she'd redressed in fresh clothes, the kitten was walking around meowing loud enough to wake the dead. It immediately climbed up her jeans to her waist the minute it spotted her.

"Crazy thing. You can't climb me like a tree. When you get bigger, your claws will hurt." She scooped him off her hip and settled him on her shoulder while she gathered his things to carry to the office with her.

Harley D kept up a steady chatter as she got ready to leave. Though he didn't have the coloring of a Siamese, the little monster *talked* like one. She found herself talking back as she double-checked that she hadn't left anything she might need.

"You have giant feet for such a tiny kitten. I bet you're going to be bigger than we think. If you grow into your feet, you're bound to be a big cat."

As she climbed the slight rise with the kitten on her shoulder and both hands full of his "things," Angela decided she would let the guys help her move the rest of her belongings over to the house after dinner that night.

"No reason to put it off. We're getting married. That's as much of a commitment as you can get."

Harley D didn't comment this time. She could hear him purr, though, and took that as his agreement with her decision.

When she walked into the office, the phone was already ringing. She hurried to answer it after dropping Harley's supplies to the floor.

"Wood's Wilderness. Can I help you?"

"Is this Angela?" a woman asked with a voice strong and demanding.

"Yes, it is. Can I help you?" she asked again, frowning.

"I'm Grace Woods, Travis and Randy's mother. I'm so glad you answered the phone. I've wanted to talk to you ever since the boys told me about you."

Angela felt her newfound self-confidence falter. She hadn't expected to have to deal with their parents so soon and certainly not without them there for support.

"Um, hi."

"Don't worry. I don't bite." Laughter filled the other woman's voice. "I just want to find out more about you. All I could get out of my boys was that you were wonderful and an amazing cook."

"Oh. Well. I'm not a chef or anything. I think they have been living off of their own cooking for so long that they are exaggerating a little."

"Although I know you are right about the extent of their skills or lack of skills in the kitchen, I've no doubt you are every bit as good as they claim. I can't wait to meet the woman my boys have finally fallen in love with. They did tell you that we're coming this weekend, didn't they?"

"Yes. They did. It will be a pleasure to meet you and your husbands." She had no idea what to say to this woman.

Grace sounded like a force of nature that could blow in and control everything and everyone in her path. Angela didn't know yet where she stood with this woman. Hopefully she would like her and not hold her background against her. There was always the worry that no woman would ever be good enough for her sons in her eyes.

"I can tell you're nervous, Angela. Don't be. We aren't coming to judge you. We're coming to meet the future mother of our grandchildren and help you plan the wedding."

"Oh." Her stomach performed a perfect backflip at the mention of grandchildren.

"What I originally called for was to let y'all know that it will be Saturday afternoon before we get there. Burt, one of my husbands, is going to be tied up for a while Saturday morning handling some business, so we'll get a late start. Don't expect us before two or three in the afternoon."

"I'll tell Randy and Travis. Do you need to speak to them? I can get them on the radio."

"No, don't bother them. Oh! Almost forgot. We're planning to stay in the cabin, so tell them to make sure those damn goats they insist on keeping are penned up somewhere. I swear they have it in for me for some reason."

She heard a full-out laugh in the background then someone with a deep voice that reminded her of Randy said, "Could be because you talked about roasted goat for Christmas last year, Grace."

"Oh, shut up, Mark." Grace's voice sounded muffled as if she'd put her hand over the mouthpiece. "Anyway. You take care of yourself and don't let them work you too hard. You'll need your rest for when I get there. We have a lot to do. Bye, dear."

Grace disconnected, leaving Angela feeling as if the whirlwind she expected to feel once they arrived had already passed through. She stared at the phone still in her hand and slowly replaced it in the charger. It took her a few seconds to calm her jittery stomach as she sat down behind the desk. Harley had jumped down earlier when she'd dropped his things on the way to grab the phone. Now he climbed into her lap and notified her that he needed something.

She tried to put the phone call behind her and concentrated on setting up Harley's area before getting down to work. Since she was obviously going to be busy with Grace for several days, she decided that she needed to make sure everything was as caught up as possible. Randy and Travis had warned her that their parents tended to stay almost an entire week when they visited. With the threat of planning their wedding in the air, Angela wouldn't be surprised if that turned into two weeks this time.

Lunchtime snuck up on her before she realized it, and the guys walked into the office startling her into shrieking and scaring Harley D in the process.

"Sorry, honey. We didn't mean to scare you. I thought you heard us calling you when we came in." Randy grabbed the kitten and settled it in his arms, stroking his head absently.

"That's okay. I guess I was concentrating harder than I realized. I'm sorry I didn't have lunch ready for you." She jumped up to head to the kitchen to make sandwiches.

"Forget it, Angel. You don't have to fix us lunch all the time. We're perfectly able to make them ourselves." Travis stopped her and pulled her into his arms.

"Yeah, it's the one thing we can do that doesn't involve cooking something on the stove. Can't mess them up." Randy grinned before leaning over and kissing her cheek.

"Bet you're hungry though." Travis gave her a quick kiss on the lips before pushing her toward the door. "Let's go eat. Then we need to talk."

"Talk? About what?" Angela asked, worry creeping in again.

"Just stuff. Like setting a date for the wedding and moving you in and stuff like that," Randy said.

"Oh, well, I thought we'd move my stuff over tonight. I don't really have that much to move."

She could tell she'd surprised them by the way their mouths dropped open then quickly closed. Then Randy pulled her away from Travis and swung her up and around, hugging her to him before letting her slide back down to stand on her own once again.

"That's great, honey!"

"Besides, your mom called and said they planned to stay in the cabin. Um, she said they would be late getting here because one of your dads has some business Saturday morning. She said to expect them around two or three in the afternoon instead."

"Bet Burt finally found a buyer for that Mustang he rebuilt," Travis said, looking at his brother.

Angela caught the warmth in both men's smiles as they talked about their dads and how Burt liked to work on old cars and Mark trained horses used mainly as therapy horses. Their parents were semi-retired from ranching but still kept horses, and the men had their hobbies to keep them busy and out of their mother's hair. She listened to them as they ate and realized that their family had been so much different than her own.

Where Randy and Travis's family life appeared to have been close and where they were all open with each other, hers had been much more reserved. Although she and her mom had been close, they hadn't discussed anything and everything like Travis and Randy had growing up. Her father had loved her, but he'd been a strict man, expecting her to follow the rules and learn to be a good housewife like her mom.

When she'd lost her parents, Angela had relaxed some and finally pursued the education she had craved so she wouldn't be stuck with her only option being to get married. And here she was about to get married after all. She couldn't stop the smile from breaking through at the thought of spending the rest of her life with Randy and Travis. Somehow the idea of keeping house for them didn't sound all that bad after all. She guessed love had a way of softening anything that once appeared harsh.

"I like that smile, honey." Randy took the plate from her hands and rinsed it before adding it to the dishwasher.

"Come on. Let's go get comfortable in the living room so we can talk." Travis pulled her away from Randy and the sink.

She let him draw her into the other room and situate her on his lap in his recliner. He nuzzled her neck, nipping at it while they waited for Randy to join them. She moaned when he sucked at her earlobe. It didn't take much to arouse her with them. She could already feel the wetness between her thighs as her pussy heated up.

"No fair. You left me in the kitchen just so you could hold her." Randy pouted as he dropped into his chair.

"You can hold her in a minute," Travis said with a chuckle.

"Don't fight over me or I'll sit on the couch—alone." Angela grinned as Travis growled behind her.

"We're not fighting over you. We're negotiating who holds you first."

Randy rolled his eyes at his brother's response. Angela couldn't help but laugh at his expression. This was what she had hoped for when she finally met the man she married. What did it matter if there were two of them? Obviously there were others who felt the same way.

"Okay. Seriously, Angel. We need to decide when we are going to get married so that we can let our parents know. Randy and I say the sooner the better, but we know you'll want to plan a wedding, and that takes some time. Just remember, we don't plan on waiting forever though." Travis kissed her cheek as she leaned back against his chest.

"I really hadn't thought about planning a wedding. I thought we'd just go to the judge and get married or something." She hated the thought of the expense, and since she didn't have any money or parents to pay for the wedding, it would fall on Travis and Randy to pay for it.

"I wish!" Randy hooted with laughter. "There's no way mom will let us do that, honey. You might as well resign yourself to planning a wedding. If you don't want anything elaborate, then put your foot down with her, but I know our mom and she's going to insist on a wedding of some type."

"Oh." Even Angela heard the disappointment in her voice.

"Hey. It won't be that bad. Why don't you want a nice wedding?" Travis squeezed her gently.

"I don't really know anyone. It just seems like a waste of money, and I can't even help pay for it."

"Don't worry about the money, Angel. As for not having friends, what about the women you met at the cookout? You seemed to get along with them well enough," Travis said.

"I just met them. I don't really know them yet." She didn't want to think about it anymore. "I'll work it out with your mom one way or another. When did you want to get married?"

She could tell that Travis and Randy were looking at each other from the frown on Randy's face. She'd said something wrong again.

No matter how hard she tried to do and say the right thing, she always managed to screw up. She sighed.

"I know it will take some time to plan the two ceremonies, so how about the first weekend in August?" Travis asked.

"Two ceremonies?"

Angela had forgotten about there being two. Naturally with her marrying one brother officially the other one would want to be recognized as her husband as well. The second ceremony was all about their commitment to each other as a unit and announcing it to everyone.

It wasn't that she didn't long for a nice wedding. Like most women, Angela had once dreamed and planned hers out in intricate detail, but two weddings with no one she really knew very well attending either one was just plain depressing.

Stop feeling sorry for yourself, Angela. I have two men who love me and want to make me happy. I don't have to have a room full of people on my side when I have them.

Still, it would have been nice to have had even one friend to support her. She wouldn't even have a maid of honor or any bridesmaids outside of Travis's and Randy's sisters. Suddenly she felt overwhelmingly lonely, something she'd never felt before. She missed her parents and wished they could have lived to attend her wedding.

Hearing a sound, Angela looked up and met their eyes, realizing that she was being silly. The weddings were one-time events that she probably wouldn't even think much about once they were over. She would have her men by her side for the rest of their lives. What more did she need?

A fairy godmother, maybe—and luck. Lots of luck. They said that they loved her just like she was, but when all the new and shiny wore off, would they still feel the same way?

Chapter Eighteen

"Yeah, remember? You'll marry Travis on paper in the official wedding and then we have a smaller ceremony where we all three pledge ourselves to each other." Randy smiled, standing up.

He walked across to where she sat on Travis's lap and knelt down beside the chair to look into her eyes. He could see the anxiety churning there. Tension fairly leapt off her skin. He hated seeing her worried like that.

"I–I had forgotten." She forced a smile across her lips, but Randy could tell it wasn't natural.

"Don't worry about it, baby. Mom will help you. I think she's been planning for all of our weddings since we were born. At least that's what Dee Ann and Lauren tell us. I think that's one reason why they haven't gotten married yet," Travis said with a chuckle.

"My turn, Travis." Randy stood up and picked her up from Travis's lap before he could stop him.

He carried his precious fiancée over to his chair and sat down with her across his lap so that he could see her face and she could see both him and his brother. She still appeared to be a little uneasy around them. It bothered him—a lot. She should be completely comfortable around them, able to talk to them about anything. The fact that she wasn't and didn't feel that she could confide in them proved that they still had a long way to go in earning her trust. They might have earned her love, but until she completely trusted them, she was not completely theirs.

He ran his hand lightly up and down her arm, hoping to help her to relax. Having her there in his lap proved to be a sweet torture he hadn't expected. His cock hardened beneath her slight weight. As much as he wanted to adjust himself, he didn't want to draw her attention to the fact that he was aroused. Right now they needed to focus on something other than sex.

"You didn't say if the first weekend of August would be okay with you or not, honey," he said.

"Um, sure. I mean as long as it's okay with your parents that is. I don't see why we need that long anyway. It's only June. That's like a month and a half away." Her pretty blue eyes appeared wider than usual to him.

"I have it on good authority that a proper wedding takes time to prepare for." Travis grinned across at them.

"Whose authority would that be?" Randy asked.

"Mom's, you idiot. She's told us that over and over all our adult lives. Do you not listen at all when she lectures us?" Travis asked, frowning.

Randy grinned though he knew he was blushing some, too, by the warmth that spread up his neck.

"I listen to the first few seconds then I sort of tune her out. It's usually something we've heard a dozen times over the years anyway."

"Randy! I'm going to tell her you said that." Angela stared at him in mock horror.

It was worth the blush to see her teasing him. One small step. He'd take each and every one of them.

"If you tell on me, I'll torture you for hours." He grinned at her.

"Torture me? How?" Her voice broke on the *how*.

"He'll suck and lick your pretty pussy without letting you come while I hold you down, Angel," Travis said.

When she looked back at him as if to see if he really would, Randy stuck out his tongue and wiggled it suggestively before licking his lips. She shivered, and he swore he could smell her arousal. He ached to slide his hand down the front of her jeans to see if she was wet. He wanted to strangle his brother for bringing sex back into the conversation. How was he ever going to be able to keep his mind off of sinking his cock deep inside her tight ass or that hot, wet pussy if Travis kept making suggestive comments?

"Let's talk about some rather boring subjects for a while," he said glaring across at his brother. "Do you want to trust Harley D's safety with Homer and his wife while we're gone on our honeymoon or should we ask Mom and the Dads to stay here and kitty sit for us?"

"Speaking of honeymoon," Travis interrupted. "Where would you like to go? We figure we can take a week away from the ranch, so where would you like to go?"

"Honeymoon? I–I hadn't thought about going anywhere. Um, Homer and his wife can take care of Harley D if they don't mind. Where do y'all want to go? I wouldn't know how to choose. I've never really been anywhere other than the trip to here."

Randy couldn't concentrate on what she was saying for watching her lush lips as she spoke and stealing glances at how wide her blue eyes got with each question. Travis really was in for it when he got him alone again. Keeping her off balance wasn't getting them anywhere. As long as she stayed flustered, she wasn't truly thinking about them as a ménage, a family. He wanted her to get used to them in that context.

"Don't you have dreams of going somewhere special, Angel? What do you dream about?" Travis asked.

"I don't know. Mostly I've dreamed about getting a good job and a place of my own." Angela's features softened with a small smile.

"Well you have both of those now. You're doing a great job in the office and now you have a home here with us." Randy patted her hip lightly.

Travis seemed to finally catch on to what Randy wanted to accomplish with her that afternoon.

"You can decorate it any way you want to. We really haven't done anything to the house other than update the kitchen and bathrooms.

The colors and stuff are all like it was when we bought the place. All you have to do is tell us what you want, Angel."

Randy nodded. "It's your home as much as it is ours, honey."

Angela smiled. "Okay. Would you mind if I polished the wood floors? They're really pretty, but they need taking care of."

Randy groaned. "Angela. You don't have to ask our permission to do something. Maybe if you're thinking about changing something major we could all talk about it, but something like that is up to you."

He could tell she was struggling to accept that she wasn't just their employee anymore. Maybe it would take more time after all. He probably should be thankful that she'd agreed to marry them in the first place knowing how she felt about their being her bosses first.

The sound of Harley D's yowling meow from the direction of the office had Angela scrambling off his lap before he could stop her.

"I'd better go check on him. He's not used to being by himself for long periods of time yet." She soon disappeared into the entrance hall. He could hear her crooning to the kitten before the office door closed once again.

"What the fuck are you trying to do, Travis? I thought we were going to try to get her comfortable with us so she would confide in us more." Randy stood up, stuffing his hands on his hips and glaring at his older brother.

Travis sighed and stood up as well. "She's already agreed to move her things on over tonight. That's a big step. I think pushing her too much at one time will only cause her to clam up tighter. She's still holding something back, and I for one want to know what it is. We can't find out if she's busy analyzing her feelings. We have to keep her off balance so she slips up. Once she gets whatever it is out in the open, *then* she'll start to relax more."

Randy scoffed at his brother's method of solving their problems with their soon-to-be wife. He might be older, but he wasn't the all-knowing Wizard of Oz on women. God knew they'd both screwed up with Belinda. First she'd driven them crazy wanting them to take her shopping all the time, and then she'd tried to pit one against the other by wanting to marry only one of them.

"I think you're reading too much into her nervousness. All she's worried about is the fact that she's sleeping with her bosses and is going to be marrying them. It's guilt over that that you're picking up on. She's not keeping some big secret from us, Randy."

"You're wrong, brother. There's something she isn't telling us that has her feeling guilty. That's why she's so jumpy around us and is trying to keep some distance between us."

Randy stuffed his hands into his pockets. "But she's not doing that now. She agreed to move in with us."

"Doesn't mean she isn't still holding back. I don't care what's in her past. I still love her, but she needs to be honest with us. If our relationship isn't rooted in honesty, it will fall apart the first time we come up against something major." Travis obviously wasn't budging from his decision.

Randy knew from past experience it was better to back off and let him have his way than to keep baiting and arguing with him. Still, it worried him that Travis's bulldog tendencies would eventually lead to greater problems.

"Fine. Just remember that she's a human being whose sense of self-worth is rooted in what she can do for someone. If she thinks she's not everything we want her to be now, she's liable to run."

"It won't come to that, Randy." Before he could say anything more, the office door opened and Angela emerged from the entrance hall carrying the kitten.

"He was hungry. I guess he'd eaten all his food and thought his food bowl should never be empty. I refilled it, and he ate two bites then wanted me to hold him." Angela's grin was infectious.

Randy smiled and walked over to pluck the scrawny ball of fur from her arms. He held the well-loved kitten up to his face and stared into his eyes. The little bugger hissed at him.

Angela burst out laughing then gasped and covered her mouth as if she'd messed up. Travis started chuckling behind her, and she joined in once again. Randy frowned at both of them before hugging the kitten to his chest and petting it. When it settled down and started to purr, he stuck his tongue out at them.

"He forgot for a second who I was is all. I'm the one that always made sure they had extra food and milk."

"No, he just hadn't been that close to your ugly mug before and it scared him. That's all. It wasn't until you moved him out of sight of your face that he started purring again. Face it, little brother, you scared him."

"Travis. That's not nice. He hisses at me sometimes, too. Don't listen to him, Randy. He's being mean." Angela reached and took Harley D out of his arms to snuggle the kitten against her breast, where he wanted to be.

"Okay, you guys. I've got to get back to work. If I'm going to entertain your mom this weekend, then I've got to finish up in the office." Angela turned and walked back out of the living room.

"We'll see you tonight, honey," Randy called after her.

"Love you, baby." Travis added.

"I love both of you, too!"

Randy smiled. Things were going well.

Chapter Nineteen

Travis pulled off his gloves and stuffed them in his back pocket. Finally all of the hay had been relocated to the newer barn they'd built. The old barn needed work, and moving the hay had been the first step toward emptying it so they could replace the rotten wood and repaint it. Next came the tools, spare parts, and just plain junk that had accumulated over the years. Some of it dated back to the first owners who'd left it when they'd sold the place.

"Damn, I can't wait to get a shower tonight. I've got fucking hay all over me. It even feels like it's in my damn jeans." Randy stomped out of the barn, jerking off his gloves.

"I hear you. Wonder what Angela cooked tonight?" he wondered out loud.

"Hmm, whatever it is, we both know it'll be delicious." Randy brushed off the hay that clung to his clothes with his gloves.

"Damn phone. It's been vibrating all afternoon."

"Why haven't you answered it? It could have been important." Randy straightened up.

"I don't recognize the number, and it's a text anyway. The hands would have used the radio and Angela would have called or used the radio as well." He sighed and pulled the offending thing out of its holder and scrolled through the many text indications to find the first one.

He was anal that way. He wanted to read from the beginning if he was going to look at them. When he pressed to open it, a picture of Angela talking to Jace Vincent opened up. Angela looked nervous, Jace intense. The next text was a message.

Looks like your girlfriend has another boyfriend.

He frowned and pressed the next message. Another picture popped up. This time Jace had his hand on her arm. The deputy looked interested to Travis. He couldn't stop the growl from slipping out.

"What's wrong?" Randy moved closer.

"Just a minute." Travis wanted to read them all before he said anything to his brother.

A sick feeling was building in his gut. Had this been why she'd been acting so strange the day before? Did she feel guilty for seeing Jace when she'd been sleeping with them?

Bet you thought you could trust her, didn't you.

He selected the next text and another picture opened up. His stomach sank even as his anger grew. Angela was in the deputy's arms, her face turned away so he couldn't see her expression. Jace's expression was easy to read. He liked holding her. Travis cursed and nearly threw the phone across the ranch yard. Instead, he scrolled down to the last message.

I wonder what else she's been doing.

Travis gritted his teeth as he fought to keep from crushing the phone in his hand. Randy was standing next to him, waiting for him to let him see. He didn't want to show the damn thing to him, but he needed to know. Why couldn't he have been wrong? Anger at the pain he would see on his brother's face when he looked at the damning texts burned his gut. Finally he handed the phone over to Randy and waited.

"What the fuck?" His brother looked over at him after he'd looked at the first message.

"Just keep scrolling," was all he could say.

After several long seconds, Randy handed his phone back to him. Instead of the pain he'd expected to see, there was denial instead.

"It doesn't mean anything. Jace is a good man. He'd never screw around with someone else's woman."

"Maybe he doesn't know she's ours. It's not like we've broadcasted our intentions, and she's only been here for a little over a month." Travis could see Randy's confidence crack.

"We need to ask her about it before jumping to conclusions. I don't believe she'd jump into someone else's arms straight out of ours."

Travis scowled. "You think I want to believe it? It's there in black and white. She played us, Randy. Made us think she was shy and didn't feel right getting into a relationship with her bosses, and we fell for it."

Randy shook his head. "There has to be another explanation. I can't believe these pictures are what they look like. I have to see it with my own eyes."

Travis wanted to yell at his brother for being so stubborn about it. Instead he ground his teeth and stomped toward the truck. They would confront her about the pictures and see what she had to say for herself. Then maybe his brother would acknowledge that pictures don't lie.

Randy climbed up in the passenger's side as Travis threw the truck into gear. Neither man said anything on the drive back to the house. Each had too much on his mind with one small woman at the center of it all. Travis had seen her as their miracle, an angel on the side of the road with beautiful, sad eyes he couldn't resist. He'd brought her into their lives, believing she'd prove to be the glue that would bind them into a family and that he and his brother would be whole once more.

He growled as they pulled up at the house. A deputy sheriff's SUV sat parked beside the blue truck out front.

"Aw, hell." Defeat and betrayal echoed in Randy's words.

Travis cursed as he jumped down out of the truck. He stopped before he slammed the door. He didn't want them to know they were there if they didn't already. He wanted to surprise them and see how they reacted. Thankfully Randy didn't slam his door either.

He gestured to his brother that they were going to go in the back through the kitchen. Trace slipped around the back with Randy right behind him. They eased into the laundry room then walked quietly across the kitchen. When he looked into the living room, no one was there. Listening carefully, he could hear the murmur of voices coming from the office. Looking over his shoulder, he nodded at Randy and they carefully made their way across the wood floor of the living room to the entrance hall. The office door was closed.

Travis grasped the doorknob and drew in a deep breath. Letting it out in a slow, controlled stream, he opened the door wide and froze. Randy's *fuck* beside him sounded loud in the suddenly quiet room.

Angela's eyes widened even as she struggled to pull free of Jace's embrace. For his part, the deputy appeared worried, as well he should. Travis stepped into the room, ready to pound him into the ground. Randy moved with him even as Angela cried out and ran past them with tears streaming down her face. He ignored her and focused on the object of his immediate anger.

Jace held up both hands, palms out, as if to ward them off. Travis wasn't buying what he was selling. Red-hot rage burned in his blood as he swung at the other man. Jace sidestepped him, but Randy managed to land a solid punch to the man's jaw. Jace was a big man. The blow staggered him, but he didn't go down. Instead he tried to talk.

"Wait. It's not what you're thinking. Nothing is going on."

Neither of them was listening to him. Trace ran at him with the sole purpose of taking him down. Jace managed to evade the brunt of the hit, sidestepping to the side of the desk. With both he and Randy after him, he really didn't have anywhere to go.

"Stop! I'm trying to tell you that nothing is going on. I was worried about her. She looked sick in town yesterday." Jace raced around the desk but Randy headed him off.

"Yeah, we saw how you were checking on her," Randy said in a growl.

"She looked like she was going to pass out. I just came out to check on her. She looked scared yesterday like something was wrong." Jace tried again to talk to them.

Randy managed to shove him up against the wall. The other man didn't even try to fight him this time when Randy pulled back his fist to hit him.

"You're fucking this all up, guys! Angela loves you two. Now she thinks you don't trust her." Jace's much louder voice stopped Randy's fist from moving.

Travis didn't believe him. He wanted to pulverize Jace for taking what was theirs. Still, the devastation he'd briefly seen on Angela's face as she raced by them had him listening to the deputy.

"I swear. There's nothing going on between us. I saw her on the sidewalk in town yesterday and was worried about her. She looked like she was about to pass out, but when I stopped to check on her, she assured me she was fine. She was shaking though. Then I saw her later at the diner and she tripped and almost fell. I caught her before she could hit the floor. It was obvious to me that she wasn't all right, but I couldn't do anything about it when she insisted nothing was wrong."

"Why did you come out here? You know she would be safe here with us." Travis didn't want to believe him.

"Honestly? I wondered if something was wrong out here. She acted like she was afraid of something. I couldn't stop worrying about her last night, so I drove out here to check on her. What you saw just now was just her confessing that she loves you both very much, but she's afraid she's not good enough for you. She thinks that in a few months or years you'll regret that you married someone like her."

"What the fuck does that mean?" Travis asked.

"It means we haven't convinced her that we love her because of who she is. She's still scared that she isn't good enough for us." Randy's words made some sense.

"She told me that she'd decided to trust the two of you to know what you wanted and what sort of person she was until your mom called and then she started worrying that she was making a mistake again. Guys, she needs your unconditional love, not this mistrust you're showing her." Jace's words made sense, which pissed Travis off.

Jerking back from the other man, he watched as his brother released Jace and stepped back as well. The deputy straightened his shirt and nodded at them.

"You better go see about her before she ends up hurt."

Randy was already walking out of the room as Travis nodded at the deputy. Then his brother's curse had him hurrying to the entrance hall.

"What?" he asked.

"She's not wearing shoes. Her boots and tennis shoes are right here in the hall," Randy said, pointing to them.

"Damn. She's going to cut her foot or break an ankle." Travis threw open the door.

"I'll help you look," Jace said. "We can cover more ground with three of us looking."

Travis nodded at the other man as he and his brother surged through the front door one after the other. He had a bad feeling again.

* * * *

Angela stumbled down the rise as she stepped on rocks and fallen limbs. Tears blurred her eyes to the point she could barely see.

Having run out without bothering to stop and pull on her boots or even her tennis shoes, she was paying the price with stone bruises and sore ankles. At least she still had on her socks.

Despair poured over her once more as she thought about how Randy and Travis had looked when they'd opened the door into the office earlier. Travis's eyes had been furious even as his mouth curled into a snarl. Randy's expression of disappointment and maybe even regret had nearly brought her to her knees. That they hadn't even bothered to give her the benefit of a doubt hurt her beyond measure.

I knew it wouldn't last. They already think the worst of me and we aren't even married yet. How could I have been so stupid?

Angela stumbled once more as anguish over losing the two men she loved more than anything else squeezed her heart in a vise grip. She'd been right in the first place. Falling in love with them had been foolish. Now she'd gone and done what she'd been afraid of to begin with. She'd lost her heart and her job.

Her foot slid off a rock twisting her ankle so that she stumbled again. This time she didn't find anything to hold on to and fell hard on her knees. Pain splintered along her knees and down her shins. Grabbing a low branch of one of the scrub bushes, she managed to remain upright on her knees. Short nubs on the branches dug into her hands like sharp needles. How much more would she have to endure before she made it to the cabin? She looked up from her position on the ground. Nothing looked familiar. Had she wandered off the path? Panic flared through her as she scrambled to her feet, desperate to locate a familiar landmark.

Just as she stepped forward, the sound of rattles froze her in mid-motion. Afraid to even move her head to try and locate the snake's position, Angela fought to stay focused. She couldn't afford to freak out now. Her very life might be at stake depending on where the rattler was in relation to her unprotected feet and legs.

Because she had just come from that direction, Angela had to trust that behind her was safe. Instead, she slowly forced herself to look around in front of her, turning her head very slowly so as not to startle the snake. To her left, she finally spotted the menace not three feet from her left foot. It looked to be a good three feet long as well even though it was curled with its triangular head lifted in threat. Hadn't she read somewhere that they could strike as far as the length of their body?

What was she going to do now? Her legs and hands already ached and stung from falling so many times. Could she throw herself to the opposite side fast enough to keep the deadly fangs from making contact with her skin? Fear began to eat away at her until panic threatened to take over her thought processes. If she panicked for real, she might do something exceedingly stupid.

A noise behind her had her jerking, and the snake's rattles grew louder as its irritation grew. Angela couldn't stop a new wave of tears rolling down her face. They blurred the image of the snake, which only frightened her more.

"Easy, honey. Don't move. Everything is going to be okay." Randy's deep voice washed over her taking away some of her fear.

"What do I do? He's going to bite me, isn't he?"

"No. He's not. We're going to get you out of this. Trust me, Angela."

She could hear the pleading in his voice as if he knew she was still contemplating lunging to one side.

"Travis. Grab a rifle and hurry over to where the path to the cabin veers off to the right if you're not careful. Be quiet though. A snake has Angela pinned down." Randy's voice was low as he talked to his brother.

Angela couldn't hear Travis's reply, but she knew he would even now be coming to help. Even if they no longer wanted her, they were good men and wouldn't want to see her die no matter how badly she'd screwed up.

The sound of someone approaching ratcheted up her anxiety as the snake once again began shaking his rattles. Just as suddenly, the slight noise stopped as whoever it was stopped moving.

"Hell. That doesn't look good. I'll move to the other side so I can get a shot."

That was Jace's voice she heard. At least they hadn't all killed each other over her stupidity.

"Travis is on his way with a rifle. He should come out at the right angle to pop it. I don't want you to spook the damn thing by moving. Hold off a second and let's see if my brother can take care of it. The rifle will be a more accurate shot than your pistol." Randy's voice sounded so calm to her.

Angela could feel the tremors start in her legs as she grew tired of holding the slightly uncomfortable position for so long. How much longer until Travis got there? She wasn't going to be able to stay still for much longer. The tremors turned into fine shakes. Even her teeth were chattering now.

"Easy, Angel. I'm here. Don't move, baby." Travis's voice was a welcome sound because it meant he would have the rifle and her ordeal would soon be over.

"Just stay real still, honey. Travis will kill it and everything will be fine." Randy sounded so far away now. She wondered if he was leaving already.

A strange ringing in her ears seemed to be drowning out everything around her. She couldn't even hear the snake's rattles anymore. She thought she heard Randy's voice but couldn't be sure. It sounded like he was telling Travis to shoot the damn thing already. The next thing she knew, the world around her tilted and she was falling even as a burning sting flared along her calf.

Chapter Twenty

"Travis! Take the damn shot! She's going to pass out."

Travis heard the desperation in his brother's voice. He didn't have a clear shot from his present position, but if he didn't take it now, the snake would strike when she fell. Hell, more than likely she would end up falling on the damn thing. That would be a death sentence. The fucking snake would strike over and over again if she did.

All of this went through his mind in the blink of an eye as he lined up the sight on the rifle with the snake and took the shot as she pitched forward, directly toward the snake. He cursed and hurried over to pull her off the fucking reptile even as his brother and Jace reached her first. He covered them with the rifle so that when they jerked her off the snake, if it were still alive, he would kill it.

To his relief, the snake's head had been severed from its body, and though the body still twitched on the ground, the head was nowhere near his angel now. He still kicked the head out of their way and focused on Angela. Her bloody legs and hands reminded him that they had screwed up by jumping to conclusions. Well, he'd been the one to jump. Randy had only reluctantly followed him. Not only had he put her in this situation, he'd fucking grazed her with the bullet as well. She would never forgive him at this point.

Dropping the rifle to the ground, he knelt beside his brother as he and Race dabbed at her cuts and abrasions and tied a cloth around her lower leg where he'd shot her.

"Angela, baby? Can you hear me? I'm sorry. I'm so sorry," he whispered as he ran a hand through her hair.

"Let's get her to the truck, Travis. She needs the doctor. I want to be damn sure she doesn't have a snake bite somewhere we might have missed." Randy's voice was thick with emotion.

"I'll go start the truck while you bring her." He grabbed the rifle once more and ran toward the house where the trucks were parked.

Dear God. Please let her be okay. I can't stand the thought of her being hurt. Especially when it's all my fault.

He had the truck turned around and the passenger door open when Jace and Randy appeared carrying Angela. As soon as Randy had her secured in his lap with the seat belt around them both, Travis took off down the drive behind Jace, who had the lights, flashers, and siren going on his vehicle to clear a path for them.

"She's going to be okay, Travis. I can't find that the snake got her anywhere." Randy's words did little to reassure him.

"I fucking shot her, Randy. Hell. I'm the reason she ran out there without boots on in the first place." His knuckles whitened as his grip on the steering wheel grew tighter.

"You didn't do any such thing. We both screwed up how we handled this. And if you hadn't taken the shot when you did, she would probably be dead by now. That rattler would have filled her full of venom before we could have gotten her away from it."

Travis didn't say anything more. Instead he struggled to remain calm so he didn't wreck them on the way to the hospital. There would be plenty of time for self-flagellation later. Right now, he needed to make sure Angela didn't hurt anymore. Something he should have been thinking about instead of believing the worse, that she was hiding something bad from them instead of her fear that she wasn't good enough for them.

How would they ever be able to get her to trust them again? Forget them, him? He was the one to blame for all of it. Why when he had been the one to bring her into their lives had he been the one to doubt her the first time they faced trouble? Hell, he was the one who had warned his brother not to screw things up by believing the worst.

"Why isn't she waking up?" Randy questioned as he stroked his hand down her arm.

"I don't know. Did she hit her head on anything when she fell?"

"I couldn't find any swollen areas or blood in her hair or around her face."

Travis risked a quick glance at her and frowned. She was pale, and her eyes were sunken as if she'd been sick. Was she sick and they hadn't noticed it? That was unacceptable. They should have been focused on her, making sure she was happy and healthy. How had they screwed this up so badly? Their parents would be ashamed of them. They'd been raised to always watch out for a woman, be it their sisters, their mother, or a friend's wife.

"We're almost there, Randy." He wanted to reassure his brother, but words failed him.

The presence of Jace's SUV with flashing lights ahead of them was making all the difference in how fast they could drive and the lack of traffic slowing them down. He owed the man an apology and a big thanks. He wouldn't forget it. Glancing toward Angela one more time, he promised her and himself that if she would give him another chance, he would prove to her that he loved her and would never doubt her again.

* * * *

Angela woke up to a burning pain in her left leg as well as stings and aches all over her palms and knees. What had happened to her? She struggled to open her eyes even as she grasped at vague memories. Suddenly it all came back to her, and she gasped for breath even as she tried to move. Her eyes flew open.

"Whoa, Angela. Be still, honey. We're on our way to the hospital. You're just fine." Randy's voice did little to soothe her fears of having been bit by the snake.

"It bit me! I'm going to lose my foot!" She tried to look down her body to see her leg and almost screamed at the sight of a section of someone's shirt wrapped around her bloody leg. What had they done, cut it and tried to remove the venom?

"Calm down, Angel. You're not going to lose your foot. It didn't bite you," Travis said.

She jerked her head up to look at where he sat stiff as a board driving the truck. He looked too upset and nervous. They weren't telling her something. They were lying to her. She was sure of it. She remembered feeling the sting as it buried its fangs in the side of her leg.

"Don't lie to me!" She knew she was yelling, but she couldn't help it.

"Calm down, Angela. We're not lying. The snake didn't bite you. Travis accidently winged you when he shot the snake. He killed the snake, but you were so close that the bullet grazed your leg. You're going to be just fine." Randy sounded so calm despite the worry on his face she saw when she gazed up at him.

Slowly she started to calm down. Her breathing eased back to normal as her heart rate decreased one beat at a time. She felt as if she'd been run over and dragged across rocky ground. It seemed as if every inch of her body hurt somewhere. As the overwhelming fear receded, the pain picked up and the adrenaline rush gave way to weariness. She closed her eyes once again.

The next time she opened them, they were pulling up at the entrance to the emergency room of a hospital. The passenger door was thrown open, and a young man dressed in green scrubs reached for her as Randy unbuckled the seat belt. He took her from Randy's arms and laid her on a stretcher where she was immediately covered by a blanket and wheeled toward the sliding doors to the building.

She could hear voices all around her talking at once. Occasionally she could pick out either Randy or Jace's voice, but she didn't hear Travis's anywhere around. For the next twenty or so minutes, the people in the room with her asked her all sorts of questions from where did she hurt, to when had she last eaten. Someone drew blood and someone else stuck an IV in her hand as they stripped her and examined every inch of her body. It all happened so fast that she didn't have time to feel embarrassed until a smiling blonde-haired nurse was dressing her in a hospital gown.

"You are one lucky woman. Snake bites can be deadly, and at best, painful. You'll be right as rain in no time with a little rest." The nurse turned to leave.

"Wait. Where are Randy and Travis?"

"They're right outside the door. As soon as they finish filling the doctor in on what happened, I'm sure they will be right in. Rest, Angela. You've had a pretty bad shock."

Angela watched the nurse push through the swinging door, leaving her alone in the small exam room. Though the head of the stretcher had been elevated slightly, she still couldn't see her legs or feet. She felt something tight wrapped around her left lower leg and wanted to know what it was. She still harbored the fear that she really had been bitten by the snake and they weren't telling her yet.

Slowly she took inventory of her many aches and pains to find that she had an IV in her left hand, the mystery bandage around her left lower leg, another bandage on her right knee and a plethora of cuts and sore places all over her body. She felt tears forming in her eyes once more and struggled to prevent them from falling. They wouldn't help a damn thing, and she'd cried enough today already.

A whoosh of sound had her jerking her head toward the door. Randy and Travis walked in and stopped next to the stretcher wearing worried expressions. Angela didn't know what to do or say. She was sure they were angry with her for what they would have seen as cheating on them. She didn't know what to say to explain to them that she hadn't been cheating. Would they even believe her if she tried.

"Th–thank you for saving my life." She included them both in her glance.

"Honey, there's nothing we wouldn't do to protect and keep you safe. I'm so sorry for how we reacted when we walked into the office this afternoon. It was unforgivable that we jumped to conclusions like we did." Randy's deep voice sounded so good to her ears.

She wanted to believe him, to believe that they believed that she hadn't been cheating on them. She looked over at Travis and felt her heart break at the pain in his eyes. It didn't look like he shared his brother's thoughts on the situation. That hurt. She wanted him to trust her and care about her as much as she loved them.

"Travis?" Her voice broke on his name.

He seemed to fall in on himself as he stepped closer to the stretcher and reached out to run a single finger down her cheek.

"I'm so sorry, baby. I was a fool. I should have trusted you instead of believing you were keeping something from us. We should have all talked about whatever was bothering you instead of letting it simmer and bring us to this, with you getting hurt. I'm sorry I shot you. I couldn't get a clear shot, but if I waited, you would have been bitten for sure." Tears seemed to shimmer in his chocolate eyes.

"It's all my fault for not talking to you both. I was afraid you would be disappointed in me if I told you how I felt." She reached up with her free hand and clutched at his, trapping it against the side of her face.

"Nothing is your fault, honey. We were supposed to be taking care of you and we failed. I swear if you give us another chance it will never happen again. Let us prove to you how much we love you, Angel." Randy dropped his hand to the top of her head and rested it there.

"Y–you still want me?" she asked in shock.

"Of course we do, baby. You're our angel. You mean everything to us." Travis smiled a shaky smile as he bent and kissed her lightly on the lips.

She wanted to pull his head closer and devour his mouth, but he held one hand in his and her other hand was anchored down by the

IV. He pulled back far too soon for her taste. She whimpered at the loss of his taste.

Randy kissed her next, but he, too, backed away far too soon.

"Rest, baby. We're right here. We're not going anywhere without you." Travis continued to hold her hand as she closed her eyes once more.

* * * *

"She did what!" Travis's angry voice woke her.

"Keep it down, brother. You're going to wake her up. Let's step outside." Randy's voice sounded just as angry as his brother's but was much quieter.

"I'm already awake. What's wrong?" Angela looked over to where Jace, both of her men, and the sheriff, Mac Tidwell stood near the door.

"Nothing's wrong, Angel. We'll take care of it. Go back to sleep, baby." Travis had obviously tried to regain some control over his anger, but it still bled through in his voice.

"Don't keep something from me, guys. I mean it. We have to be honest with each other or this isn't going to work. Remember?" she asked.

Randy and Travis both had the grace to blush as they sighed in union. She knew she had won, but the obvious smile on the sheriff's face made her mad.

"Don't you dare laugh at them. I'll tell Bethany on you."

His quick sobering expression affirmed that Bethany was a force to be reckoned with in their family. She smiled at him and turned back to her guilty-looking men.

"What's going on?"

"Um, we just found out who sent us some rather suggestive pictures of you with Jace when you were in town the other day," Randy said.

"Pictures? What pictures?" She didn't remember anything about them receiving pictures. "I sorted the mail and there weren't any envelopes large enough to hold pictures addressed to either of you. What are you talking about?"

"Someone sent pictures to our cell phones suggesting that you were cheating on us. When we showed up at the house to talk to you about them, we found you in Jace's arms and jumped to conclusions. We're so sorry, baby." Travis once again looked a bit sick.

"I want to see the pictures," she said, not believing that they could look half as incriminating as they implied. She hadn't done anything wrong with Jace.

Travis pulled out his phone and moved closer to the bed. He pressed on the screen a few times then handed it over to her. She read the first message before scrolling down to the first picture. Okay, it wasn't all that bad. They were just talking. The next message and the next picture was a little more damning. It was the third picture that would have sealed the deal. It was when she'd tripped and Jace had kept her from falling on her face. That one looked bad.

Angela closed her eyes before holding out the phone toward Travis. "I can see why you were so upset to begin with when you walked into the office. I'm so sorry. I…"

Randy interrupted her. "You have nothing to be sorry for. You didn't do anything wrong. We're the ones who should have stopped to question the validity of the photos. We should have asked questions first when we walked into the office before attacking Jace."

She waved her hand in the air to stop him from continuing. "Let's not get into this again now. Who sent the pictures?" She wanted to know who her enemy was.

"It was Belinda." Jace was the one to answer her. "We traced the call to a disposable phone that we found in a dumpster behind the diner. The thing is, the stupid idiot bought the phone here in town not thinking that someone would remember that she'd bought it. Plus, we managed to lift a fingerprint off of it that matches hers we got off a glass at the diner a little while ago."

"She's not going to leave it alone, guys. She wants Randy, and she'll keep causing trouble between us." Angela felt as if the happiness she'd only briefly held in her heart was being snatched away from her again.

"No, she's not." The sheriff smiled. "It seems her parents are so embarrassed by her latest shenanigans that they are shipping her off to live in New York with her aunt. If she doesn't go and stay there, they threatened to rewrite the terms of their will so that she couldn't have access to her money until she was thirty and married. That was all it took to get her packing her bags. She flies out of Dallas tomorrow morning bright and early."

Angela couldn't help but smile. Maybe everything would work out all right after all. She reached over the bedside rail to grasp Travis's hand. Randy shuffled closer and rested his hand on her shoulder before leaning over to kiss her gently on the lips.

"I'm sorry for everything that's happened, Angela." Randy brushed his lips across hers once more.

"We're going to leave you guys alone now." Jace's voice reminded her they had an audience and were still in the hospital emergency room.

"When can I go home, guys?" she asked.

They stiffened above her for a brief second then relaxed. "We're taking you home with us as soon as the nurse returns with your discharge papers. The doctor said you had to take it easy for a few days, but that you're going to be fine." Travis grinned down at her.

"You have three stitches in the side of your leg, Angela, so you're going to have to behave and stay off it for a few days to let it heal up." Randy winked at her.

"We think we know just the way to keep you in bed, too." This time Travis winked at her.

She was sure her face had changed to a brilliant shade of red from the amount of heat that burned there. Naturally, the nurse chose that moment to return with papers for her to sign. She listened as the woman ran through the instructions for taking care of her stitches while she removed the IV from the back of her hand. Then she signed the papers and was relieved that they were going to give her a pair of scrubs to wear home since they had cut up the other clothes she'd been wearing getting them off of her.

"You know, I think you need some new clothes, Angel. We'll have to plan a shopping trip as soon as you're well enough to shop again." Travis grinned at her.

Randy grinned at her. "Don't worry, honey. Mom will insist on taking you herself so Travis won't be allowed to help you change in the dressing room like he is planning."

Angela couldn't stop the chuckle of pure joy that escaped when she caught sight of Travis's scowl at that news. She would have to watch out for that one. It was obvious that he had a bit of naughtiness hidden inside of him. For some reason, that bit of information didn't scare her one bit. If anything, Angela's blood rushed through her veins even as she felt her panties dampen. She might find out that she liked a little bit of naughty with her men just fine.

Chapter Twenty-One

Once they returned home, Travis carried her up to the bedroom and settled her in while Randy returned to her cabin to move everything over to the house. In three days, their parents would be arriving and expected to stay there while they visited. Angela couldn't be happier to be with her men all the time now. She still had to remind herself over and over that they loved her regardless of where she'd come from, but she was working on it.

Friday night, Angela lay in bed bored out of her mind after Harley D had finished his visit with her and was once again banished to the laundry room. She was so tired of staying in bed she could scream. There was no reason she couldn't go downstairs and sit for a while. The instructions from the hospital said she could walk short distances on her leg after the first twenty-four hours. It was Friday for goodness' sake. She should be able to go dancing by now if she wanted to.

Finally she decided she'd had enough and had talked herself into making her way downstairs on her own. She would sit on the couch for a while and watch TV. The change of scenery would be good for her. Randy had offered to put a TV in the bedroom for her while she was recovering, but she hadn't wanted to get in the habit of watching TV in bed. It was a practice she'd always detested. The bed was for sleeping—and other things, not for watching TV.

Angela listened hard to see if she could detect either of her men downstairs. Hearing nothing suggesting they were still in the house, she eased off the bed onto her good leg and carefully walked across the room to the bathroom. After cleaning up some, she grabbed a robe off the back of the bathroom door and slipped into it. The thing swallowed her whole, but she figured it would work fine to keep her covered. The short T-shirt of Travis's was large enough to cover the most important parts of her, but she preferred to have her legs covered as well in case of company.

She hitched the length up and held it out of the way as she carefully walked across the room and through the door. Pausing at the top of the stairs, Angela made sure she didn't feel dizzy before she started the long slow journey down the steps. Once at the bottom, she sighed with relief and continued into the living room. There she picked up the remote to the TV and sank thankfully down on the comfortable couch, letting the robe cover her legs as they stretched out on the cushions.

At some point, she found an interesting documentary about the ancient Egyptians and eventually fell asleep. The sound of a door closing behind her jarred her awake and for a second she wasn't sure where she was. The sound of Travis's voice and then Randy's brought a smile to her face as she remembered. As they grabbed beer out of the fridge, the two men talked about a cow that had tried to outmaneuver them. She could listen to them talk about their day for the rest of her life.

She greeted them with a smile on her face when they walked into the living room and saw her reclining on the couch. Her smile faltered some when both men frowned and slowly stalked toward her.

Uh-oh. Maybe I shouldn't have come downstairs by myself after all. They look angry.

"What in the hell are you doing down here?" Randy asked with a soft growl in his voice.

"Who the fuck helped you get down here?" Travis didn't sound much calmer.

"I was tired of lying in bed all alone up there. I got bored." She knew she was pouting but hoped it would soften their anger some.

"I offered to put a TV up there for you," Randy pointed out.

"I know. But I'm tired of that room. There's no reason I can't sit down here and watch TV." She poked her lower lip out for effect.

Travis shook his head and stood over her with a dangerous-looking twinkle in his eyes. Angela knew she should be worried about that expression, but instead, she felt her body respond with a strange sort of excitement.

"Randy. I think she's healed enough that we can carry on with her punishment now."

"Punishment. For what?" A thrill shot down her spine to lodge in her pussy.

"We were to blame for everything that happened, baby, but make no mistake that you weren't totally innocent, Angel. You should have trusted us enough to talk about what you were feeling." Travis shook his head.

Randy bent over her and picked her up. She let out a squeal as he gently tossed her over his shoulder. His hand came down heavily on her upturned butt.

"Hey!" she yelped.

"What do you think, Travis? Ten or fifteen for not confiding in us?" Randy asked as he headed toward the stairs.

"Put me down, Randy!"

"I think ten for not telling us what she was worried about and another ten for taking a chance and coming downstairs alone today. She could have fallen down the stairs and seriously hurt herself." Travis's voice came from below her as Randy started up the stairs.

"You're not going to spank me twenty times!" Angela couldn't believe what she was hearing.

"Hmm, she's talking back, too. Maybe we should add another five on for that," Travis added.

"I like how you think, brother."

When they reached the top of the stairs, Randy walked faster toward the bedroom as if he couldn't wait to lay into her. Angela couldn't believe they would enjoy spanking her like that. Sure, she wouldn't mind an occasional game of it, but not for real. She screeched when Randy suddenly moved her off his shoulder and sat down with her across his lap.

"Are you going to be a good little angel and take your punishment or do we need to tie you down?"

"You are *not* tying me down to beat me!" She tried to get off his lap, but one hand held her there at the small of her back.

Travis bent down next to her and kissed her cheek. "Now, now, baby. Don't tempt us, angel."

Then someone threw the hem of the robe over her head and a large, warm hand caressed her ass cheeks. It had to be Randy's hand by the feel of the size of it. She dropped her head and sighed. Obviously they were intent on punishing her. She wasn't going to fight them over it. She'd kept things from them, and that had started the entire incident in the first place. She could handle a spanking. She didn't really believe they would hurt her.

Randy's hand came down on her ass cheek in a stinging slap twice. Then she felt blunt fingers gently fingering her pussy. The next sensation to her stinging ass cheeks was a warm, wet mouth laying kisses over the burning, licking away the slight sting left there from Randy's earlier slap.

Angela couldn't stop the moan that escaped her lips as those blunt fingers slowly slipped deeper inside her already-slick pussy. She wanted to rock back on them but was afraid to move in fear they would disappear.

"I think twenty orgasms are a good start to her punishment, brother." Randy's deep voice sounded even rougher now.

She curled an arm around his lower leg to hold herself still even as her body wanted to move back against the fingers moving in and out of her cunt. As much as she wanted their cocks filling her, she wasn't about to throw away a climax at their hands. Those were good, too.

"What do you think, baby? Do you deserve twenty orgasms?"

"Please." She couldn't get anything else out of her mouth as another finger slowly dragged some of her juices from her dripping pussy back toward her dark hole.

"Let's move her over to the bed, Randy. I've got to taste her," Travis said in a raspy voice.

Randy picked her up and pivoted to lay her gently face-first on the bed. He lay down beside her and took her lips in a slow, sensuous kiss that seemed to stop time. His tongue licked along the seam of her mouth to plunge inside the instant she opened to him.

Her legs were spread wide as Travis settled himself between them. She felt odd lying on her stomach, but soon forgot all about it as Travis stabbed her pussy with his stiffened tongue. He fucked her with it once, twice, then circled her aching clit and proceeded to lap at her juices as they seeped from her body. Each touch of his mouth at her pussy burned a need for more deeper and deeper until her cunt quivered with the need for a hard, hot cock to fill it.

Once again he collected her pussy juices with his fingers to smooth over her anus. As he sank one thick finger into her pussy, he pressed another one into her ass, one slow inch at a time. The pressure was exquisite even as she fought to press back against him to take more of him inside of her. She wanted—needed more, so much more. Angela wanted to once and for all belong wholly to them so that there was never any doubt in her mind or theirs that she did.

"Take me, Travis. Oh, God! Take me."

"Come for me first, sweet angel. Give me your pleasure." Travis added a second finger to her throbbing pussy before latching onto her clit with his devilish mouth.

The direct stimulation to that ball of nerves proved to be more than she could handle. Fire raced through her body as his questing fingers slid back and forth over her hot spot deep in her cunt. The draw of his mouth at her clit added to the pleasure that engulfed her.

"Yes!" She couldn't stop the scream that followed as everything around her disappeared in a warm fire that burned her from the inside out.

When she slowly returned to reality, it was to find herself on top of Randy with his long hard dick pressed at her entrance. As if all he'd been waiting on was for her to regain awareness, his eyes captured hers just before he sank deep inside her still-quivering cunt. Swollen tissue parted to accommodate his girth, adding another level of burn to simmer within her.

"Fuck, Angela. You're so damn hot and tight."

His words seemed torn from him as he hissed when she sank down the last inch of his cock, mating their bodies as close as they could get to each other and still remain separate.

All she could see and feel revolved around Randy as he pumped his dick into her body, pulling her down as he pressed up. Each thrust seemed intent on branding her as his. The fierce expression on his face could have been frightening if she couldn't see the emotion in his eyes. There was lust, yes, but there was love and even adoration in the fire of his hazel eyes. Angela would never be able to doubt his feelings for her again. This was what they needed, this intense coupling that bound them together, all three of them.

Angela turned her head to find Travis watching them, appreciation and passion etched deeply into his features. She reached back to include him in the moment that was their pledge to their relationship. His feral smile assured her he would be joining them soon even as he gently pushed her down to relax over his brother's chest.

"You are the most beautiful creature I've ever seen, Angela," Travis whispered behind her.

She felt his hands as he smoothed them down her back to caress her buttocks. The rough calluses of his fingers sent shivers across her body. A pop followed by a cool drizzle of lube down her crack alerted her to his intentions even as he massaged it into her back hole with his finger. The press of first one, then two deep inside her ass was a welcome pinch and burn. More lube soon made the press of his fingers in and out of her little rosette easier. She pushed back against his fingers, wanting him to hurry and replace them with his thick cock.

The snap of the cap on the lube along with the withdrawal of his fingers warned her that his cock would soon be replacing them. She ordered her body to relax as Travis spread her ass cheeks wide and guided his dick to her stretched opening. The first press of his spongy cockhead burned and pinched as the broad cap breached her, sending a burning fire through her body.

"Hell, you're so tight. I'll never last." The words seemed almost torn from him as he pressed forward.

Randy had gone still, giving Travis time to slowly enter her. Neither man wanted to hurt her. If she knew nothing else, it was that they would never willingly harm her in any way. Even now, Travis strained to remain in control so he wouldn't accidently hurt her. She wanted more, though, and she didn't want wait one more second for it. Angela slammed back against his cock, driving him all the way inside of her even as she yelled out.

"Fuck! Angela, baby." Travis stilled inside of her and laid his forehead against her back. "Are you okay? God, did I hurt you?"

"No. Fuck me, Travis—Randy. I need you to move. Now!" She groaned, holding on to Randy's shoulders as the men slowly moved around her.

As Randy pulled out of her, Travis pressed in, and then they switched directions and Randy was filling her cunt with his cock. Their cockheads dragged over swollen, sensitive tissues, sending shards of electricity zinging throughout her body. Each rasp as they stroked inside of her tightened her pussy and hardened her clit to the point of pain. Travis's cock inside her ass had nerve endings sizzling that had never known pleasure before.

Pleasure and pain built until she no longer could tell the difference. It all morphed into an unending need for release. She whimpered with it, begging to come. She didn't know if she was asking out loud or only in her head, but she desperately needed to come.

"Randy. I can't hold on much longer. She's so fucking tight." Travis seemed a million miles away.

Randy pressed his fingers against her throbbing clit and tapped at it over and over. The splendid pressure ignited a fuse that sped hot and fast toward something she wasn't sure she was ready for. Both men began pounding into her as if they couldn't get close enough to her. She no longer moved between them, instead letting them control her as they alternately and sometimes together filled her with their straining cocks.

Then everything exploded in a burst of light and intense heat that seemed to swallow everything to the point that she couldn't see, hear, or feel anything but an unbelievable rapture. It consumed her even as it remade her. She would never be the same. Somehow she knew this even as sound and sight came rushing back at an overwhelming pace.

Angela whimpered as she once again felt Randy beneath her and Travis behind her, heavy against her back. She fought to breathe around the pressure of his weight.

"Travis. Fucking move, man. You're suffocating us both down here." Randy's amused voice didn't sound as strong as she was used to hearing.

Travis grunted but slowly pulled out of Angela and sank to one side. He didn't lose contact with the skin of her back though. He kept one hand smoothing along her spine even then. It comforted her and reminded her that they loved her, loved her despite and because of who she was. Never again would she doubt their sincerity.

"I love you, Travis, Randy. I will always love you." She managed to draw enough breath to tell them what was in her heart.

"I love you, Angela. You are truly our angel," Travis said.

"You are my everything, Angela. We will make it our life's mission to show you each and every day how much you mean to us." Randy's rough voice softened when he said her name.

"How about a shower, guys?" Angela asked.

"When I can move again," Randy moaned.

"Me, too," Travis added.

"Randy! Travis! Where are you keeping that angel of yours?" The voice calling up the stairs had all three of them sitting straight up in bed.

"Fuck! That's mom. What are they doing here?" Travis asked as he scrambled to climb out of the bed.

"Hey, guys. Your mom wants to meet Angela. You better get dressed and get down here before we lose our grip on her."

"That's Burt. If he says we better hurry, we better hurry," Randy said with a groan as he pulled on his jeans.

"I'm taking a shower first. I'm not meeting your parents right after having had sex, guys. You can keep them busy until I come down." Angela headed for the bathroom but was stopped by a hand on her wrist.

"You better not waste any time in there or I'll come get you and haul you downstairs buck naked if I have to," Travis said with an evil grin.

She kissed him then grabbed Randy and kissed him, too. She wasn't even worried about what their parents thought about her anymore. All that mattered was that her two men loved her. She could handle anything with that knowledge in her heart.

THE END

WWW.MARLAMONROE.COM

ABOUT THE AUTHOR

Marla Monroe has been writing professionally for about ten years now. Her first book with Siren was published in January of 2011. She loves to write and spends every spare minute either at the keyboard or reading another Siren author. She writes everything from sizzling-hot contemporary cowboys, to science fiction ménages with the occasional bad-ass biker thrown in for good measure.

Marla lives in the southern US and works full-time at a busy hospital. When not writing, she loves to travel, spend time with her cats, and read. She's always eager to try something new and especially enjoys the research for her books. She loves to hear from readers about what they are looking for next. You can reach Marla at themarlamonroe@yahoo.com or visit her website at www.marlamonroe.com

For all titles by Marla Monroe, please visit
www.bookstrand.com/marla-monroe

Siren Publishing, Inc.
www.SirenPublishing.com

CPSIA information can be obtained
at www.ICGtesting.com
Printed in the USA
BVOW09s1226221017
498319BV00006B/59/P